SHARED IN PUBLIC

An Ordinary Couple's Journey Into
Swinging and Submission

Scarlett Duffy

Copyright © 2025 Scarlett Duffy

All rights reserved

The characters and events portrayed in this book are fictitious. Any similarity to real persons, living or dead, is coincidental and not intended by the author.

No part of this book may be reproduced, or stored in a retrieval system, or transmitted in any form or by any means, electronic, mechanical, photocopying, recording, or otherwise, without express written permission of the publisher.

CONTENTS

Title Page
Copyright
Prologue
The Invitation — 1
The Arrival — 14
The Challenge — 42
The Moment Of Truth — 59
The Instruction — 75
The Host's Duties — 83
The One More — 109
The Morning After — 140
The Return Visit — 155
The Moment After — 184
The Final Steps — 192
The Final Moment — 220
Books By This Author — 225

PROLOGUE

Steve lay awake, staring at the ceiling, his mind tangled in the memories of the past weekend. It had only been a few days since they'd returned home, slipping back into the quiet routine of their normal lives, but nothing felt the same.

Not after everything they had done.

Beside him, Beth was sprawled across the sheets, her body bare, her skin glowing with a post-orgasmic sheen. She was utterly spent, lost in the deep, dreamless sleep that always followed their most intense nights together. His gaze drifted down, lingering on the soft curve of her hip, the slight parting of her thighs.

She was still messy.

A pearlescent trail gleamed faintly in the dim light, seeping from her swollen folds, sliding down the inside of her thigh, vanishing into the rumpled sheets.

But this time, Steve wasn't sure who he was seeing when he looked at her.

He knew exactly what that sight reminded him of.

Beth beneath Tommy.

Beth spread wide, taking every thick pulse of another man's cum inside her, her moans echoing in Steve's ears even now.

He swallowed hard, his pulse quickening at the thought.

He had watched her. He had seen everything. And worse—he had enjoyed it.

But how much of that pleasure had come from watching her lose herself? How much had come from knowing he had no control, that Beth had given herself so completely to someone else?

His stomach clenched, the same strange mix of arousal and unease curling in his gut.

He had thought coming home would put some distance between them and what had happened. That time would let him sort through it, make sense of it.

But here they were, back in their own bed, and Beth still looked exactly like she had that night. Wrecked. Used. Spent in a way that was no longer just his doing.

A sleepy murmur escaped her lips as she stirred, shifting slightly. When she moved, she felt it—that hot, sticky mess still clinging to her, the sheets damp beneath her. A slow, lazy groan slipped from her throat, her body stretching languidly, completely unbothered.

"Yikes, I'm so messy," she mumbled, her voice thick with exhaustion and satisfaction.

The same thing she had said that night.

Steve's fingers clenched into the sheets.

Beth sat up, swinging her legs over the side of the bed. She cupped a hand between her thighs as she stood, catching the warmth that pooled against her palm before padding toward the bathroom with that familiar, exaggerated waddle.

He watched her go.

Watched the sway of her hips, the casual ease in the way she carried herself.

She wasn't conflicted.

She wasn't dwelling on anything.

Maybe she had already accepted it. Maybe it hadn't left the same knot in her chest that it had in his.

Or maybe—just maybe—she was waiting for him to say something.

His gaze flicked back to the ceiling, his breath leaving him in a slow, heavy exhale.

How long before they did it all over again?

And did he want them to?

THE INVITATION

Steve and Beth arrived at Chloe and Rich's home around five the previous afternoon, the golden light of early evening stretching long shadows across the quiet suburban street. The visit had been arranged on a whim, born from one of Beth and Chloe's infrequent but always engaging phone conversations.

Chloe had called, as she often did, to catch up, her voice bright with mischief and familiarity. Steve, lounging in his usual easy chair, half-listened as Beth recounted the highlights of their week, her voice shifting from casual amusement to something more hesitant near the end of the call.

"I don't know, we have so much to do here," Beth said into the phone, her tone faltering slightly. A moment of silence followed, then a small laugh—rich, knowing, indulgent.

"Well, you know we'd love to see you two, but..." she added, trailing off.

Steve watched his wife carefully. That tone—that hesitation—was something he recognized all too well. His senses sharpened as he studied the way she clutched the phone just a little tighter, the subtle way she bit her lip. Whatever Chloe was suggesting, it had planted a seed in Beth's mind, and he had a strong suspicion of what it was.

A sudden burst of laughter escaped Beth's lips, light and flirtatious. "You're a devil, you know that?"

Another pause. This one longer. Beth nodded absently, listening, her expression unreadable. The tension in the room thickened, and Steve could practically hear Chloe's voice weaving its persuasive magic through the phone line.

Then, with a sigh and an exaggerated shrug, Beth finally relented. "Oh, what the hell, why not?" she said, her voice carrying a note of both resignation and intrigue. "We could sure use a change of pace. So, yes, we can come next weekend, I guess. Let me just check with Steve."

She turned, placing a hand over the receiver, her eyes meeting his with a glint of something unspoken. Temptation. Anticipation. A challenge.

"They want us to visit next weekend," she murmured, her voice softer now, more intimate. "You know what they probably have in mind. So… do you want to go or not?"

The air between them was charged, expectation hanging thick. Steve held her gaze for a long moment, already knowing the answer even before he spoke.

Frankly, Steve was shocked to hear the excitement in his wife's voice. They had been friends with Chloe and Rich for a long time, their connection built on years of laughter, shared experiences, and playful flirtation. The four of them had partied together, indulging in just enough teasing and boundary-pushing to make things interesting. The wives, emboldened by alcohol and the thrill of provocation, had taunted the men with their revealing outfits, dancing close, brushing against them in ways that felt deliberate. It had always been a game—an unspoken dance at the edge of temptation.

Then, one evening, Rich had confessed what Steve had long suspected: he and Chloe were occasional swingers. The revelation had hung in the air like a loaded gun, a truth waiting to be acknowledged, even acted upon. There had never been any overt pressure—just subtle invitations, lingering glances, and the way Chloe's hand would sometimes rest on Steve's knee just a fraction too long.

Now, Chloe's invitation for a weekend visit carried a different weight. Unspoken, yet unmistakable.

Steve glanced at Beth, watching the way she absently ran a hand through her hair, her fingers grazing the nape of her neck. Her body language gave her away. There was a hesitation, but beneath it, there was something else—something new. Interest. Curiosity. Maybe even desire.

Beth and Chloe had always been close, but Beth had never been able to fully accept Rich. She had confided in Steve more than once that she sometimes felt he mistreated Chloe, that his charm was a thin veil over something colder. And yet, despite those reservations, here she was, considering it. For the first time, she seemed ready to take the next step.

The thought sent a bolt of arousal straight through Steve's core.

His gaze lingered on his wife, her delicate features, the soft curve of her lips. Then, his mind betrayed him, filling the space between reality and fantasy with a vision so vivid he nearly shuddered.

Beth—naked, her back arched, her knees digging into the mattress as she trembled beneath another man's touch. Rich, kneeling behind her, his thick, rigid length poised at her entrance, teasing her, stretching her, making her whimper with anticipation. Her hands fisted in the sheets, her lips parted in a breathless moan as she surrendered to the slow, deliberate push inside her.

A sharp breath escaped Steve before the scene in his mind shifted, replaced by another—one even more illicit.

Chloe, her wild blonde curls spilling over her shoulders, her blue eyes smoldering with mischief as she knelt between his legs. Her lips, soft and slick, parting around the head of his cock as she took him into the warm, wet heat of her mouth. He imagined the slow, torturous glide of her tongue, the way her cheeks hollowed as she sucked him deep, her hands gripping his thighs as she worked him over with practiced skill.

His pulse hammered in his ears, the hair on the back of his neck standing on end. A shiver crawled down his spine, his skin prickling with raw, unfiltered desire.

Was this really happening?

The fantasy that had lived only in his darkest, most private moments—the one he had entertained countless times, always dismissing it as an impossibility—was suddenly within reach.

His throat went dry as he struggled to find words, to mask the sheer, burning need twisting in his gut.

Beth was still watching him, waiting for his answer, completely unaware of the storm raging inside him.

Did he want to go?

God help him, he did.

"Uh, no other real plans," Steve mumbled hoarsely, still feeling the lingering heat of his thoughts. "So, I guess we could go if you want to."

Beth uncovered the phone, a slow smile spreading across her lips, her eyes glinting with something between excitement and mischief. "Steve said okay, so we'll accept your invite. We can probably be at your place by late Friday afternoon. Is that all right?"

The conversation continued for a few more minutes, shifting to meal plans and what they should bring. Steve only half-listened, still caught in the whirlwind of anticipation now swirling in his chest. The way Beth's voice softened, the way she laughed easily with Chloe—it was all a stark contrast to the hesitation she'd shown at the start of the call. Something had shifted.

By the time she hung up, Beth was giggling, her fingers absentmindedly playing with the hem of her blouse. "Chloe said to pack at least one sexy black dress. They want to take us to a new hot spot Saturday night," she divulged, her voice tinged with excitement. "Sounds like a fun weekend, huh?"

Steve smirked, leaning back in his chair, arms crossing over his chest. "It's always interesting when we're together with those two," he remarked, watching her closely. "I have a feeling old Rich has some naughty designs on you. Are you prepared for that, honey?"

Beth tilted her head, her expression unreadable for a moment, then with slow, deliberate steps, she crossed the room and settled onto his lap. Her fingers trailed lightly down his chest, teasing, testing.

"Maybe Rich is over his fixation on my tits," she murmured, her lips just inches from his, "but if you're right... are *you* going to be okay with a little fun and games?"

Steve swallowed, his throat still dry, the warmth of her body seeping into him. She was teasing, but there was something else there too—something unspoken, a challenge wrapped in a question.

Beth traced a finger along his jawline before leaning in, kissing him with a slow, sensual tenderness. The heat between them flared, but she pulled back just before he could deepen it. Her gaze searched his, waiting for something.

"I know Chloe is going to try to get to you," she said, her voice softer now. "So if you're uncomfortable at all, I'll call her back and cancel."

Steve hesitated, his mind racing as he considered his wife's words. There was an edge to her voice—a teasing challenge, but also an unspoken question beneath it. How far were they really willing to go?

He slipped an arm around her waist, pulling her a little closer, his fingers trailing over the curve of her hip before giving her soft rear a slow, deliberate pat. The warmth of her body pressed against his, and for a brief moment, he let himself imagine what the weekend might bring.

"Let's just see how it goes once we get there," he murmured, his voice low. "They might just want to fool around, like we've done before. You know how you and Chloe love teasing us, wearing those barely-there outfits, acting innocent while driving us insane." He smirked, pressing a kiss to her temple. "Maybe that'll be as far as it goes. And if it is, that's fine—because you know how it gets us so worked up. Our bedroom time after those nights is always incredible."

Beth let out a soft hum, tilting her head as if considering his words. But there was something playful in her gaze, something that told him she already knew this was going to be more than just an evening of teasing.

"Chloe mentioned they have a hot tub," she countered, running a slow finger down the center of his chest, letting it linger just below the waistband of his pants. "And she's *very* eager for us to join them for a soak." Her lips curled into a knowing smile. "You *do* realize what that might lead to late at night, don't you?"

Steve swallowed, his imagination immediately conjuring the image—Chloe and Beth submerged in the steaming water, their bodies glistening under soft outdoor lighting, the scent of warm chlorine mixing with the faint traces of perfume. Hands slipping under the bubbling water, stolen touches, Beth's bare shoulders gleaming in the moonlight as she leaned back with a soft, breathless laugh...

His pulse quickened, but he kept his expression neutral.

"Well, we're good friends with them," he said finally, the words measured. "So that won't be such a big deal... will it?"

Beth's lips parted slightly, her gaze locked onto his, as if daring him to say more.

For the first time, the unspoken possibilities between them weren't just fantasies—they were edging closer to reality.

And Steve had no idea if he was ready to resist it.

Beth sighed, finally relenting. "Probably not. Besides, I was happy to hear that Rich has been a lot more loving and attentive toward Chloe lately. She says he's really changed—that he's figured out being domineering and rude pushes people away. She told me he's like a different man now, and she's loving it."

Steve nodded, considering that. "That's good to hear," he said seriously. "I know that always bothered you. Honestly, it bothered me too. Chloe's such a sweetheart—she deserves someone who actually appreciates her."

Beth smiled softly, tilting her head as she thought about her friend. "Yeah... she really is. Beautiful, fun, full of energy. I can't blame you for showing her a little extra attention." She shot Steve a sideways glance, her tone light but laced with something deeper. "She *is* younger, after all. And let's be honest—she's got an amazing body."

Steve chuckled, shaking his head. "So do you, babe," he said, his voice warm with sincerity. "You don't see the way Rich looks at you every time we're around. He practically *drools* over you." He slid his hand over her hip, squeezing gently. "And I don't blame him. It just makes me even prouder to be your husband... and your lover."

Beth met his gaze, her expression unreadable for a moment before she leaned in, brushing her lips against his in a slow, lingering kiss.

"Good answer," she murmured against his mouth, her voice teasing, but with an unmistakable flicker of heat.

Beth slid onto Steve's lap, her bare thighs pressing against his as she wrapped her arms around his neck, pressing a wet, lingering kiss to his lips. His hand instinctively moved to her breast, cupping the soft weight, his thumb grazing over the peak until he felt it tighten beneath his touch.

"Let's shower together and retire early," he murmured against her lips, his grin full of suggestion.

Beth smirked, brushing her fingers through his hair as she pulled back just enough to meet his gaze. "Mmm, I like the way you think."

She stood, taking his hand and leading him toward the bathroom, her hips swaying just enough to keep his eyes locked on her. Steve followed willingly, his pulse already kicking up in anticipation. The warm hum of the overhead light filled the space as Beth reached into the shower, twisting the handle until a steady stream of hot water cascaded from the showerhead, steam curling around them instantly.

Without hesitation, she peeled off her clothes, dropping them carelessly onto the floor. Steve took a moment to admire her—

her toned body, the curves he knew so well, the way her skin flushed slightly under the heat of the water.

Beth glanced over her shoulder, catching him staring. "You planning to stand there all night, or are you going to join me?"

Steve grinned and quickly shed his own clothes before stepping into the shower behind her. The moment the hot water hit his skin, he let out a content sigh, but his focus quickly shifted as Beth turned to face him, her hands smoothing over his chest, fingers tracing over every ridge and hollow.

"You know," she murmured, her voice soft and teasing, "I love seeing you like this... so relaxed, so open."

Her hands drifted lower, nails grazing the taut muscles of his stomach before wrapping around him—his cock still soft, but responding to her touch. She stroked him slowly, her palm warm and slick from the water, her movements featherlight at first, barely more than a whisper against his skin.

Steve inhaled sharply, his fingers twitching at his sides as he resisted the urge to take control. But Beth wasn't going to let him rush this.

She leaned in, pressing hot, open-mouthed kisses along his jawline, then down his throat, letting her tongue flick against the damp skin. Her strokes grew more deliberate, more teasing, feeling him harden in her grasp.

"That's it," she whispered, lips brushing against his ear, "just let me take my time with you."

Steve groaned, his breath hitching as his cock thickened under her touch. She dragged her thumb over the sensitive tip, swirling the moisture around, reveling in the way he shuddered against her. The slow, torturous rhythm had him gripping the cool tile wall behind her, fighting the need to flip their positions and take her the way his body ached to.

Beth, of course, knew exactly what she was doing.

She pressed her slick body against his, her nipples grazing his chest as she tilted her head up, eyes dark with desire. "You feel so good in my hands," she purred, her strokes tightening just enough to make him curse under his breath.

And then, just as she felt him reaching that perfect point of tension, she let go.

Steve let out a frustrated growl, his hands moving to grip her waist, but Beth only smirked as she turned away from him, stepping deeper into the hot spray of water.

"Tease," he muttered, voice thick with need.

Beth glanced back over her shoulder, water droplets clinging to her flushed skin, her lips parted, her breath coming faster. She reached out, bracing her hands against the shower wall, arching her back just enough to tilt her hips toward him.

"Enough teasing," she said, her voice husky with demand. "I want you inside me. *Now.*"

That was all the invitation Steve needed.

His hands slid over her slick waist, fingers gripping firmly as he stepped in behind her. He guided himself to her entrance, rubbing the swollen head of his cock along her folds, feeling her heat despite the steady stream of water cascading over them. She was dripping wet, and not just from the shower. The anticipation had left her aching, her body already begging for him.

Steve teased her for just a moment longer, running himself along her sensitive slit, brushing against her clit, making her body twitch in frustration.

"Steve," she groaned, pushing her hips back against him. "Don't make me beg."

The sound of her voice—low, needy, laced with impatience—sent a pulse of raw desire straight through him. Gripping her hips, he pressed forward, sinking into her inch by inch, feeling her stretch around him. Beth let out a shuddering moan, her fingers tightening against the cool tile as she arched her back even more, taking him deeper.

"Fuck, Beth…" he murmured, sliding in until he was buried to the hilt. The heat of her, the way she clenched around him, was almost too much to bear.

Beth exhaled sharply, her body adjusting to the delicious fullness. "God, you feel so good," she whispered, rocking her hips experimentally, savoring the way he filled her.

Steve pulled back slowly, almost completely, then drove forward again, eliciting a gasp from her lips. He started with deep, measured strokes, dragging himself out agonizingly slow before pushing back in with just enough force to make her whimper. The contrast of the warm water on their skin, the slick heat of her body gripping him—it was overwhelming. His hands roamed over her wet curves, gripping her waist before sliding up to cup her breasts, rolling her sensitive nipples between his fingers.

Beth moaned, her back arching further, pressing herself against his touch. "More," she panted, pushing back into him, her hips matching his rhythm. "I need more."

Steve groaned, his grip tightening. He sped up just a little, rolling his hips as he plunged deeper, the sound of their wet bodies colliding echoing in the tiled shower. He reached around, one hand slipping down her stomach, fingers finding her clit.

Beth gasped at the contact, her body jerking in pleasure. "Yes... right there," she breathed, her voice trembling.

Steve circled the sensitive bundle of nerves, alternating between slow, teasing strokes and firmer pressure in time with his thrusts. Every movement sent another jolt of pleasure through Beth, her moans growing louder, more desperate. Her body clenched around him, and Steve felt himself slipping dangerously close to the edge.

But he wasn't ready to let go just yet.

He leaned over her, pressing his lips to the back of her neck, tasting the water and salt of her skin. "You love this, don't you?" he murmured against her ear, his breath hot despite the cooling mist. "You love how I feel inside you."

Beth whimpered, her body trembling against him. "Yes," she admitted breathlessly. "God, yes."

Steve increased the pace, thrusting harder now, deeper, filling her over and over until she was gasping, her hands fisting against the wall for support. He felt every little reaction, every twitch and clench of her inner muscles as she climbed higher.

Beth's breathing hitched, her body tightening like a coiled spring. She was right there, her pleasure teetering on the brink. Steve thrust into her faster, his fingers working her clit with expert precision.

"Steve—" Her voice broke as her entire body tensed, then shattered with release. A cry ripped from her throat as waves of pleasure rolled through her, her orgasm hitting her hard. She pulsed around him, the contractions dragging him toward his own peak.

Steve groaned, gripping her hips tightly as he slammed into her one last time, his own release overtaking him. He spilled deep inside her, his body jerking as the pleasure wracked through him. The water drowned out their moans, but the feeling of their bodies locked together in pleasure was undeniable.

For a long moment, they stayed like that—panting, trembling, still joined as the water continued to cascade over them.

Beth finally let out a breathless laugh, shaking her head. "Twice in one night," she mused. "At this rate, I *really* am going to need another shower."

Steve chuckled, pressing a lazy kiss to her shoulder before stepping back.

"Go get in bed," Beth said, turning to rinse herself off. "I'll be there in a minute... after I clean up. *Again.*"

Steve smirked, giving her a playful slap on the ass before stepping out of the shower, still feeling the echoes of pleasure pulsing through his body.

Beth grinned, watching him go, already knowing that this weekend was going to be anything but ordinary.

THE ARRIVAL

"Right on time!" Rich called out as he strode onto the porch, his voice booming with enthusiasm. He reached for Steve's hand, shaking it firmly before clapping him on the shoulder. "Let me help you with your things. I've got a pitcher of margaritas chilling, so we can properly kick off the weekend."

Steve chuckled, appreciating Rich's usual energy. "Sounds like you've got everything under control already," he replied, grabbing a couple of bags while Rich took the rest.

As they carried their luggage into the spacious guest room, Beth followed Chloe into the kitchen, where the air was filled with the scent of citrus and freshly cut herbs. Beth placed the small cooler she'd brought on the counter and helped tuck the appetizers into the fridge.

Chloe turned to her with a wide smile, pulling her into a warm hug before kissing her lightly on the cheek. "I'm *so* glad you guys decided to come," she said, squeezing Beth's hands. "We're going to have the best time. Just you wait."

Beth smiled back, feeling herself relax for the first time in what felt like weeks. "I brought my briefest black dress with spaghetti straps," she teased, raising an eyebrow. "Where exactly are you taking us tomorrow night?"

Chloe's eyes sparkled. "It's this new club, not far from here. Great music, low lights, strong drinks, and a *very* casual atmosphere," she said with a knowing smirk. "You'll have fun dancing and letting loose—being a little… fancy-free."

Beth exhaled, the weight of the past few months briefly pressing down on her. "Steve and I could *definitely* use a break. We've been in a pressure cooker lately, and it's taken a toll on our personal life."

Chloe leaned against the counter, tilting her head as she studied her friend. "Well, we're *definitely* going to fix that," she said confidently. "Tell you what—go get comfortable. I'll get Rich to pour the drinks and set up on the deck. The weather's perfect, and we're going to make sure you two *completely* unwind."

A few minutes later, Steve and Beth emerged from their guest room, having changed into shorts and T-shirts, both foregoing shoes in favor of the cool wood beneath their feet. The relaxed attire already felt like shedding a layer of stress.

As they reached the door leading to the deck, Steve suddenly paused, pointing to a small sign posted at eye level.

"Relax, at our place attire is optional."

Beth burst out laughing, shaking her head. "It's *so* them," she mused. "They actually made it official."

Steve smirked. "At this rate, we might already be overdressed."

She grinned, slipping her hand into his as they stepped outside, the warmth of the evening wrapping around them like a promise of things to come.

Beth felt a small wave of relief as she stepped onto the deck and saw that Rich and Chloe were dressed casually as well. Despite the playful warning on the sign, they hadn't yet taken things to *that* level—though she couldn't help but notice how effortlessly Chloe still managed to exude sensuality. Her cute white tube top clung to her body, highlighting her golden tan and the faint outline of her already perked nipples beneath the thin fabric.

Rich, by contrast, was dressed down in a battered T-shirt and shorts, his usual confident stance seeming just a touch more relaxed than Beth remembered.

"Rich, where are your manners?" Chloe suddenly chimed in, her voice carrying a playful but unmistakable edge of authority. "Serve our guests their drinks and offer them some chips and salsa. They must be *starving* after the drive."

Beth barely had time to process the command before Rich was already moving. Without hesitation, he retrieved the frosty margaritas and set them carefully in front of Steve and Beth, following up with a dish of salsa and crispy tortilla chips.

Steve arched a brow at Rich's quick obedience, his movements almost... eager.

"Why, thank you, Rich," Beth cooed, picking up her drink, her gaze flickering toward their host. She smiled knowingly as he lingered for a moment, his eyes drifting toward the subtle swells of her breasts beneath her thin shirt.

Chloe's voice cut through the moment smoothly. "Let's have a toast to our weekend," she suggested, lifting her glass. "I have a feeling you'll both find it *very* much worth the trip."

They all raised their glasses, the light *clink* of glass against glass punctuating the warm evening air. As Steve sipped his margarita, his gaze met Chloe's over the rim of his glass. There was something in her expression—a flicker of amusement, of knowing—that sent a small thrill down his spine.

"You know what we need?" Chloe mused. "Some music. Rich, go

turn on the stereo, will you?"

Without hesitation, Rich was up again, disappearing into the house. The speakers crackled to life a few moments later, a sultry Latin beat drifting onto the deck.

Beth watched him go, then turned to Chloe with a curious smile. "Rich certainly *is* attentive these days," she remarked, swirling her drink. "That's new."

Chloe smirked, leaning back in her chair. "You *are* perceptive, Beth," she said, stretching her arms overhead in a languid, almost feline motion. "Believe it or not, we've had a bit of a... shift in our dynamic lately."

Beth arched a brow. "Oh?"

Chloe took a slow sip of her drink before setting it down, her nails tapping lightly against the glass. "It turns out that Rich has discovered something *unexpected* about himself," she said, her voice taking on a teasing edge. "For years, he's been the boss at work—running things, making decisions, being in charge all day long. But here at home... we've come to realize he likes *not* being in control."

Steve exchanged a glance with Beth, intrigued.

"He *likes* it?" Beth asked, tilting her head.

Chloe nodded, her eyes gleaming. "He *craves* it," she corrected. "Turns out, all that authority at work builds up, and he needs a place to let it go. I used to wonder why he'd get so short-tempered or moody, but now I get it. He was looking for balance, even if he didn't realize it."

Beth sipped her margarita thoughtfully. "So... what? You just told him to start taking orders from you one day?"

Chloe laughed. "Not exactly. It was gradual. I started noticing that when I took the lead—when I made *him* wait, when I *expected* him to listen—it actually *relaxed* him. He started responding in a way I never expected. Then we talked about it, and... well, let's just say we've been experimenting."

Steve leaned back, taking it all in. "So, what? You're telling us that Rich is... submissive now?"

Chloe shrugged, a slow smile playing on her lips. "Not *all* the time. But at home? In certain situations? He *loves* it. And so do I."

Beth let out a slow breath, glancing toward the doorway as Rich reappeared, taking his seat once more. There was something different about the way he settled into his chair—relaxed, but attentive. Almost as if he were waiting for Chloe's next instruction.

Chloe leaned over and patted his thigh, almost absentmindedly, as if rewarding a well-behaved pet. "You'll probably notice it more as the weekend unfolds," she added, smirking. "But don't worry—you'll *definitely* enjoy the show."

"But what started this all off?" Steve asked quietly, his voice low enough that only Beth and Chloe could hear over the soft pulse of the music.

Chloe's lips curled into a knowing smile as she leaned in slightly, lowering her voice just enough to draw them in. "Well," she murmured, "we went to the club one Saturday and ran into a very *interesting* couple. *Very* attractive, very open-minded. But the real twist? *He* was the submissive one."

Beth blinked, intrigued. "Really? Like, how submissive are we talking?"

Chloe let out a soft chuckle, swirling her margarita. "Well, let's just say it was *impossible* not to notice once we got talking. His wife led every interaction. She decided who they spoke to, when he could talk, even how he stood. He followed her like a well-trained pet—eager, completely attuned to her. It was fascinating."

Beth and Steve exchanged a glance, curiosity piqued.

Chloe continued, her voice dropping even lower. "But the real moment? The one that truly changed everything for us? It was later that night, when we saw them in the private lounge area."

Beth leaned in unconsciously. "What happened?"

Chloe's smirk deepened. "His wife had him on his knees, naked except for a collar and leash. She let another man take her—right in front of him—while he *worshipped* her. We stood there watching as she sucked this *huge* cock, taking him deep into her throat while her husband—*on his knees*—had his face buried between her ass cheeks, licking her like his life depended on it."

Beth inhaled sharply, a slow heat creeping through her.

"He moaned every time she moved, every time she touched him," Chloe went on, eyes gleaming with memory. "And when the guy finally pulled her up onto his lap and sank into her, the husband just *kept* licking, desperate to taste every inch of her as she took another man inside her."

Steve swallowed hard, shifting slightly in his chair. He could practically *see* it—this man, obedient, aroused, completely surrendered to his wife's pleasure while she was being fucked right in front of him.

Beth exhaled slowly, eyes flicking to Steve before returning to Chloe. "And Rich saw all this too?"

Chloe nodded, her expression unreadable. "Oh, he saw *everything*."

Beth hesitated, then smirked. "And he liked it?"

Chloe's lips curved. "He *didn't* think he would," she admitted, "but I could tell he was aroused. He kept shifting in his seat, pretending he wasn't watching, but I *saw* him. And later that night, when we got home, I decided to test the waters."

Steve lifted a brow. "How exactly?"

Chloe leaned back, crossing one smooth leg over the other, enjoying the way they hung onto every word. "I took control in bed. Fully. I gave orders instead of suggestions, made him *wait* for what he wanted. And I made him *show* me how much he wanted it."

Beth bit her lip, intrigued. "And?"

Chloe's smile turned wicked. "And he *loved* it. More than he expected. He let go in a way I'd never seen before—no pressure, no expectations, just pure submission. That's when I realized… he *needed* it."

Beth glanced toward the house, where Rich was still inside. "So this whole 'attentive husband' thing isn't just him being polite?"

Chloe let out a soft laugh. "Not exactly," she murmured. "It's become part of our dynamic. The more I take charge, the more he relaxes into it. And in turn, I get off on it too. It's a win-win."

Beth took a slow sip of her drink, considering everything she'd just heard. The image of that scene at the club burned fresh in her mind, making her thighs press together instinctively.

"As you wish," she said finally, her tone light but laced with interest. She turned to Steve with an amused smile. "I think this could be very *interesting*, don't you, honey?"

Steve nodded, keeping his own thoughts to himself as he processed what Chloe had just revealed. The mental image lingered—Chloe standing above Rich, taking charge, making him *work* for her pleasure. It sent a pulse of something dark and thrilling straight to his gut.

Just then, the sliding door opened, and Rich stepped back onto the deck.

"How's the volume?" he asked, adjusting the collar of his shirt.

The music was perfect—just loud enough to enjoy but low enough to keep their conversation intimate.

"That's nice, dear," Chloe purred, running her fingers lightly over his arm as he passed her. "The music makes me want to do a little dancing."

Beth watched closely, noticing the way Rich's body language subtly changed—how he responded instantly to Chloe's touch, almost like he was waiting for her approval.

After several rounds of drinks and an evening filled with laughter, any lingering tentativeness between them had completely melted away. The conversation had become more animated, touches more casual, and the undercurrent of flirtation unmistakable.

"Our new club has *amazing* music," Chloe said, her voice lilting with excitement. "And they've got a shiny pole right in the corner of the dance floor. I've been learning how to use it—giving the audience a little something to enjoy."

Steve leaned back in his chair and smirked. "Now *that* I'd like to see," he said, his voice a little rougher than he intended.

Beth nudged him playfully, rolling her eyes as Chloe laughed.

"It's mostly just to tease poor Rich," Chloe admitted, swirling the last of her drink. "I like to give him a show, work him up. I've even been practicing *right here*—" she gestured toward the far end of the deck, where a gleaming metal pole stood anchored between the floorboards and the overhang.

Steve's grin widened as he followed her gaze. "You've been *holding out* on us, Chloe," he said. "Are we getting a private performance tonight?"

Chloe sipped her drink, her smile slow and knowing. "I *might*... if Beth agrees to try it too."

Beth raised a brow, considering. "I don't know... I *have* seen some pretty amazing pole routines. Do you wrap yourself around it? Or is it more... climbing?"

Chloe's lips curled into a wicked smile. "A little of both," she purred. "It's all about *how* you use it. And believe me, gripping something so long and round between your thighs can be *very* arousing."

Beth let out a soft laugh, shaking her head. "That *does* sound sexy."

Steve cleared his throat, shifting in his seat. "Wait," he said, latching onto something she'd said earlier. "You mentioned something about *rules*. What's that about?"

Chloe tilted her head, dragging her fingers along the rim of her glass as she met his gaze. "Oh, the *rules* are simple," she said coyly. "If you want to *watch*... you have to be restrained."

Steve blinked, his smirk faltering for just a second. "You mean... *tied up?*"

Chloe nodded slowly, amusement flickering in her eyes. "Exactly. It's all about building tension. If you *can't* move, if you *can't* touch, it changes everything. It makes you *feel* everything so much more intensely."

Beth bit her lip, considering the idea. "And it *works*? It really increases the arousal factor?"

Chloe leaned toward her, her voice dropping to a sultry whisper. *"Oh, honey... you have no idea."*

Steve swallowed hard, his pulse kicking up as he imagined himself bound to a chair, watching Beth and Chloe—writhing, twisting, teasing—just *out of reach.*

Beth must have sensed his thoughts because she turned to him, her smile slow and mischievous. "Any other rules we should know about?" she asked, her voice barely above a whisper.

Chloe turned her attention fully to Beth, her expression unreadable except for the glint of mischief in her eyes. "You must be restrained..." she paused for effect, letting the tension build, "*and* unclothed," she finished smoothly.

Beth's lips parted slightly, her breath catching for just a moment before she let out a slow, wicked smile. "That sounds *positively* sinful, Chloe," she purred, her fingers idly tracing the rim of her margarita glass.

Chloe smirked. "That's the only way it *works,*" she said matter-of-factly. "No touching. No interference. Just watching. I don't allow it any other way."

Beth turned her gaze to the two men, her expression shifting into something more serious—intense, even. She studied Steve first, then Rich, her voice sultry yet commanding. "Are you two willing to obey the rules?"

Rich nodded immediately, not a moment's hesitation. "Fine with me," he said, lifting his drink. "It's worth it to see the show."

Steve, however, remained silent, his thoughts swirling as he processed what was being asked of him. *Restrained. Naked. Forced to watch.*

There was something undeniably erotic about the idea, but at the same time, the thought of being *bound* in front of them all—of being completely exposed, powerless to do anything but sit and witness whatever Beth and Chloe had planned—made his stomach tighten. Was he prepared to submit to something so debasing just to watch the two women dance?

"I'm not sure I like the idea of any kind of restraint," Steve said at last, his voice slightly hesitant. "It sounds a bit… kinky."

Chloe let out a soft, knowing laugh. "Oh, Steve…" she murmured, shaking her head, her gaze playful yet piercing. "You say that like it's a *bad* thing." She leaned forward slightly, tilting her head. "It won't hurt at all. In fact…" she let her eyes drift over him, her smile turning downright devilish, *"you might be surprised at how exciting it is to be gently restrained."*

Steve swallowed, feeling the heat crawl up the back of his neck.

Chloe wasn't *wrong*.

"You should try everything at least once, right?" she added, her voice teasing but laced with something more—something that made Steve's stomach twist with anticipation.

Beth reached over and slid her hand over Steve's thigh, squeezing lightly. "Come on, honey," she coaxed, her voice smooth as silk. "I'll protect you, I promise. And besides…" She leaned in closer, her lips grazing the shell of his ear. *"Wouldn't you love to watch me learn some of Chloe's moves?"*

A slow exhale left Steve's lips. He could already *see* it—Beth's body twisting around the pole, her skin glowing under the soft lights, her movements deliberately sensual. And he'd be helpless, unable to touch, unable to intervene.

Beth pulled back, watching him carefully.

Steve exhaled. "Oh, all right, I guess," he said at last, his voice rough. "How bad can it be?"

Chloe clapped her hands together, her grin triumphant. "That's the spirit!" she said, her excitement barely contained. "And just to be clear, *you* don't get to decide how bad—or good—it is, Steve."

Beth bit her lip, fighting back a smirk.

"When do you want to do your little dance?" Steve asked, trying to keep his voice even.

Chloe exchanged a quick look with Beth before turning back to him, her grin widening. "Right now," she said decisively. "Before anyone has time to lose their nerve."

Beth laughed, already rising from her chair. "Come on," she said to Chloe. "Let's go round up the stuff we'll need."

The two women dashed into the house, giggling like schoolgirls, their excitement infectious. Steve let out a long breath, running a hand through his hair as he turned to Rich.

"This is crazy," he muttered, shaking his head.

Rich let out a chuckle, stretching his arms behind his head as he leaned back in his chair. "Yeah, it's a little nuts," he admitted, "but trust me, you're gonna find it... *refreshing*."

Steve shot him a skeptical glance. "*Refreshing*? You mean being tied up, stripped naked, and forced to watch our wives grind against a pole?"

Rich smirked. "When you put it that way, it doesn't sound so bad, does it?"

Steve exhaled through his nose, shaking his head. "I don't know, man. I've always been in control, and this..." He gestured vaguely, as if trying to make sense of the shift in dynamics. "This feels like handing over the keys to the kingdom."

Rich nodded knowingly. "That's exactly why it's *so* fucking hot." He leaned forward, lowering his voice slightly. "I fought it at first too, you know. I thought being the *man* meant always calling the shots. But then I started noticing something. The more I let Chloe take control, the more she got into it. The more *we* got into it."

Steve narrowed his eyes slightly, still unsure. "So, what? You just decided one day to hand over the power?"

Rich shook his head. "Nah, it wasn't that easy. It started small. Little things. Letting her make decisions, letting her *dictate* what she wanted instead of me always leading. At first, I did it just to see how far she'd take it. Then I realized—I *liked* it. And she loved it."

Steve studied him, watching the way his expression softened when he spoke about Chloe. There was something different in the way he carried himself now—not weak, not diminished, but *free*.

Rich leaned back again, exhaling. "Think about it, Steve. We're both guys who run shit in our day jobs. We call the shots, make the decisions, control the outcomes. That's exhausting after a while. So, when I walk through that door at the end of the day, I don't *want* to be the one in charge anymore." He smirked. "And trust me—Chloe *loves* stepping up."

Steve mulled that over, absently rolling the condensation from his drink between his fingers.

"I don't know," he admitted. "Beth's never really been the dominant type."

Rich chuckled. "That's what *I* thought about Chloe too. But you'd be surprised what comes out when you give her permission to let loose. It's not about being bossy or cold—it's about her knowing *exactly* what she wants and taking it. And once you see that side of your wife—the side that's been waiting for you to *let* her take control?" He shook his head, grinning. "It's a fucking *game changer*."

Steve let out a slow breath, the thought swirling in his head. He'd always loved Beth's confidence, her intelligence, the way she carried herself. But the idea of her *owning* the moment, of taking *him* as she pleased, of making him sit back and *submit* to her desires...

A strange heat curled in his gut.

Rich watched him carefully, smirking. "You'll see, buddy. Just let go for once. You might be surprised at how much you like it."

Beth and Chloe reappeared on the deck, their arms draped with lengths of Velcro and wide straps. The sight of the equipment sent a fresh pulse of anticipation through Steve's body, though he wasn't sure if it was nervous energy or something far more primal.

Chloe let the straps drop into a loose pile on the wooden floor, dusting her hands off before turning to the two men with a satisfied smile.

"Alright, gentlemen," she purred, "clothes off. Now."

Steve swallowed hard.

Beth stepped forward immediately, her demeanor cool and confident as she moved in front of Rich. "I'll take care of him," she said smoothly, her voice carrying just a hint of intrigue.

Steve turned his gaze toward his wife just in time to see her delicate fingers move to the buttons of Rich's shirt. She was calm, methodical, slipping each button free with a slow precision that seemed almost intimate. The way she moved—completely at ease—made something stir deep in Steve's gut.

But his thoughts were interrupted by a soft, knowing chuckle.

Chloe.

She had stepped up to him now, standing so close that he could smell the subtle traces of her perfume—something floral, seductive. When he glanced down, he realized her hands were already at his top button, poised to begin their task.

Her eyes locked onto his as she worked, her lips curving into a slow, teasing smile. She wasn't in a hurry. If anything, she was *savoring* this, taking her time as she released each button from its hole.

Steve felt his breath deepen as the fabric parted, exposing more and more of his bare chest. The warm night air kissed his skin, but it wasn't the breeze that sent a shiver down his spine—it was *her touch*. Deliberate. Slow.

The sound of Rich's belt unfastening caught his attention, but only for a second before Chloe's fingers found his waistband. His pulse kicked up as she worked open his belt, then moved to his zipper, her fingertips just barely grazing him through the fabric.

He exhaled sharply as the metallic slide of the zipper seemed impossibly loud in the still night air.

Then Chloe *dropped* to her knees before him.

Steve's breath hitched.

His shorts pooled around his ankles in a soft rustle, leaving only his thin underwear in place. Chloe's hands—warm, soft, *familiar in a way that sent warning bells ringing in his head*—skimmed up his thighs before coming to rest at the waistband of his briefs.

For just a moment, she hesitated. Not because she was uncertain —no, it was intentional.

A pause. A tease.

And then, in one smooth motion, she tugged them down, stripping him completely.

Steve stood utterly exposed, his semi-hard cock bobbing free as the cool air met his heated skin. Chloe's gaze flickered downward briefly, her lips parting just slightly before she glanced back up at him, amusement twinkling in her eyes.

Her fingers brushed the inside of his thighs as she pulled his briefs all the way down, her movements almost *too* slow, *too* deliberate.

Chloe let her gaze drop, and the moment her eyes landed on his groin, a slow, knowing smile spread across her lips.

"Hello, *Shorty*," she teased, her voice thick with amusement.

Steve stiffened—*not* in the way he wanted.

A prickle of heat crept up his neck, a familiar flicker of insecurity he hadn't felt in years twisting in his stomach. He *knew* he wasn't the biggest guy in the room when it came to length—he'd always been slightly below average in that department—but he also knew he made up for it in sheer girth. Still, the nickname sent a sharp jolt through him, even as Chloe's tone remained playful.

She tilted her head, watching his reaction, her eyes glinting with mischief.

"Step out now," she instructed, patting his hip lightly as if she were guiding a reluctant child.

Steve exhaled through his nose, stepping out of the pile of clothes at his feet, trying to ignore the way her gaze *lingered*.

But before he could respond, his attention was drawn elsewhere.

A movement in his peripheral vision—Beth, kneeling in front of Rich, just finishing her task.

His wife looked up at their host with an unreadable expression as she peeled the last of Rich's clothing away.

And there *he* stood, stark naked, completely unfazed, wearing a grin as if he *knew* exactly what was going through Steve's mind.

Steve's eyes instinctively flicked lower, and his stomach clenched.

Rich was already rock hard. *Fully* erect.

And fuck... he was *long*.

Steve had seen him naked before—hot tub nights, drunken skinny dips—but this felt different. The way Beth was looking at him, *taking him in*, made it feel *very* different.

Steve knew what *he* had to offer—thicker than most, *much* thicker than Rich—but he couldn't ignore the contrast. Beth had her eyes on another man's cock, *assessing* him, and for the first time in his life, Steve felt *exposed* in a way that had nothing to do with his nudity.

Chloe let out another soft chuckle, stepping closer until her breath was warm against his ear.

"Relax, *Shorty*," she murmured, her voice like silk laced with wicked amusement. "It's not *all* about length... though I have to admit," she added, casting a pointed glance toward Rich, "Beth seems *very* interested in the competition."

Steve clenched his jaw, his hands flexing at his sides.

Chloe wasn't *mocking* him exactly. No, this was something *else*. A test. A challenge.

And the worst part?

He could already feel himself getting *harder*.

Not fully, not like Rich—but *responding*.

And if he was being honest, he wasn't sure if it was Chloe's teasing that was doing it…

Or the way Beth's lips parted slightly as she *kept looking*.

"I think we'll put Rich in that chair," Chloe announced, tapping the sturdy wooden seat. Then she turned toward Steve, a smirk curling at her lips. "Steve, I think you'll be more *comfortable* in this lounger." Her tone was teasing, almost condescending, as if she knew exactly how vulnerable the position would make him.

Steve caught the glint in her eye and clenched his jaw.

Comfortable? Yeah, right.

He watched as Beth and Chloe worked together to settle Rich into the chair, their movements efficient, almost practiced. Beth guided him down while Chloe expertly wrapped the Velcro restraints around his wrists and ankles, securing them to the armrests and legs of the chair. The sound of the fasteners peeling apart and pressing back together filled the warm air as Rich let out a slow exhale, sinking into his restraints.

Then came the thick strap around his chest, pulling him snug against the chair.

He was completely bound now, his long, hard cock standing proudly between his thighs, utterly exposed.

Steve swallowed as he took it all in—the ease with which Rich allowed himself to be restrained, the casual way Beth adjusted the strap across his torso, as if it were the most natural thing in the world.

And then it was *his* turn.

"Steve, you'll lie on the lounger now," Chloe instructed, her voice silky, but firm.

Something in him bristled at the direct command, a flicker of resistance rising up—but before he could process it, Beth's hand pressed gently but insistently against his back, guiding him toward the chair.

"Come on, honey," she murmured, her touch firm but affectionate.

Her fingers skimmed his spine as she led him forward, a light but undeniable pressure that sent a small shiver through him.

Beth barely had to push before he allowed himself to lower onto the lounger, sitting on its edge. He felt *ridiculous*—completely nude, half-hard, with two women smirking down at him like he was a piece of plaything.

And then Chloe was on him again.

She knelt beside the lounger, lifting his legs onto the cushioned surface with a firm grip, her fingers grazing over his calves, her nails lightly scraping the sensitive skin. Beth was right behind her, pressing gently on his chest until he stretched out fully, his arms resting at his sides.

For a moment, he thought about resisting.

But Beth leaned down, her breath warm against his ear. "Just let go, Steve," she whispered. "Relax."

And somehow, that was all it took.

The straps came next—first around his wrists, the wide Velcro circling his arms and securing them to the lounger. His ankles were next, spread just enough to leave him open and exposed but not uncomfortable. Chloe made quick work of the last strap, wrapping it across his chest, pinning him fully.

Steve took a slow breath, testing the restraints.

No give.

He was *completely* immobilized.

Beth and Chloe stood back, admiring their work, their eyes flicking between the two restrained men.

"Perfect," Chloe murmured, stepping over to Rich.

Beth moved to Steve's side, her fingers trailing lightly over his collarbone as she leaned in, her lips hovering just above his.

For a moment, she hesitated—drawing out the anticipation—before pressing a slow, deep kiss to his mouth.

Steve felt his body react instantly, his cock twitching against his thigh as Beth's tongue teased his. There was something surreal about being restrained beneath her, completely helpless to pull her closer or deepen the kiss. It was maddening.

Across from them, Rich let out a low groan as Chloe did the same, her lips claiming his, her hands smoothing over his chest.

When Beth finally pulled away, her eyes sparkled with something he couldn't quite place—excitement, arousal… *power.*

Chloe straightened, glancing between them with a satisfied smirk. "Well," she purred, "it's clear you two aren't *going* anywhere."

Beth chuckled softly, running a hand down Steve's stomach, stopping just short of his growing erection.

Chloe turned to Beth, a glint of mischief in her eye. "Shall we give them a *show?*"

Beth tilted her head, feigning consideration before flashing Steve a wicked grin.

"I think they've earned it," she said smoothly.

Steve swallowed hard, his pulse thundering in his ears.

This was happening.

And there was *nothing* he could do to stop it.

"Turn up the music, Beth," Chloe said, her voice dripping with anticipation. "I feel like moving with the rhythm."

Beth smirked and crossed to the nearby speaker, twisting the volume knob just enough to let the slow, sultry beat pulse through the deck, setting the perfect atmosphere.

Chloe ran her fingers down the length of the metal pole, her touch light and teasing, as though she were caressing a lover. She let her fingertips glide over its smooth, cool surface, her nails barely grazing it.

Then, gripping the pole with one hand, she stepped away, letting her hips sway hypnotically to the beat, her body moving with effortless sensuality.

"Watch closely, Beth," she murmured over her shoulder, her gaze flicking toward her friend. "You'll be up next when I'm done."

Beth folded her arms, her lips curving as she leaned against the railing, her eyes flicking between Chloe's performance and the two restrained men.

Steve and Rich were utterly captivated, their gazes locked on Chloe's every move.

She twisted her body around the pole, pressing her breasts against the cool metal, her lips parting as a shiver ran through her. She rocked her hips forward, rolling them against the pole in a slow, deliberate rhythm, her movements designed to tease, to torture.

With effortless grace, she dropped into a deep squat, her toned thighs flexing as she sank low, pressing her pelvis against the metal before dragging herself back up, the friction making her moan softly—whether for effect or genuine arousal, no one could tell.

She turned, facing them now, spreading her legs slightly as she rested her hands on her hips. Her lips curled into a wicked smirk as she let her fingers trail down her stomach, stopping just above the waistband of her tiny shorts.

Steve's breath caught as her hips undulated, her movements slow and deliberate, her dampening fabric clinging to her every curve.

Her nipples were stiff, pressing against the thin white tube top, the fabric doing little to hide how much she was enjoying putting on this show.

She dragged a teasing hand up her body, cupping her own breast before pressing it against the pole, her eyes never leaving the two bound men.

Steve tugged against his restraints, instinct taking over, his pulse hammering in his ears.

Chloe licked her lips. *She saw.*

She *knew* the effect she was having on him.

And she was just getting started.

Rich's cock was now fully erect, standing tall against his stomach, veins pulsing along its impressive length. He was definitely *well-endowed*, long and straight, thick enough to be notable—but *not* as thick as Steve.

And that's what made Steve's stomach tighten.

Because while he'd always been proud of his own girth, he knew that, in terms of sheer *size*, Rich had the edge when it came to length.

Steve tried not to dwell on it, tried to shift his focus, but the way Beth's gaze lingered on their host's cock made it impossible to ignore. He *knew* she'd seen Rich naked before—hot tubs, drunken skinny dips—but this was *different*.

She wasn't just seeing it now.

She was *studying* it.

Comparing.

And fuck... Steve was *hard too*.

His own cock had risen stiff and thick against his stomach, the weight of it familiar, but no matter how rigid he got, the reality remained the same—his was *shorter*, and everyone could see it.

Chloe had been watching the whole thing unfold, the smirk on her lips growing as she took in both men's reactions.

She gripped the pole, arching her body around it, rolling her hips in a slow, hypnotic rhythm. Her movements were deliberate, indulgent, a performance designed to tease and *torture*.

And then, as she twisted her body again, pressing her bare skin against the cool metal, her tight white tube top *slipped lower*.

The soft swell of her breast peeked out, followed by the tight bud of her pink nipple.

Rich inhaled sharply, his cock giving an involuntary twitch.

Beth exhaled, her lips parting slightly as she flicked her gaze between Chloe's exposed skin and the stiff erection in front of her.

Steve felt his own pulse hammering in his ears.

And then came the moment that sealed it—*the moment Chloe fully owned them both.*

She licked her lips slowly, dragging her fingers over her bare breast, rolling her nipple between them. Then, with an exaggerated motion, she *leaned down* and licked herself, moaning softly against the stiff peak.

Rich groaned.

Steve *throbbed*.

And before he could stop it, *there it was*—a glistening bead of precum forming at the tip of his cock, undeniable proof of how much she was getting to him.

Chloe *saw*.

Beth *saw*.

And *Beth smiled*.

Not in a mocking way. Not even in an overly amused way.

But in a way that told him she *noticed*—that she *knew* his body's reaction, that she was *registering* the difference between him and Rich in real-time.

And that drove Steve crazy.

Chloe smirked, adjusting her top with a slow, deliberate motion, sliding the fabric back over her breast.

"That's all for now, boys," she purred, walking between them, *knowing* exactly what she'd done.

She passed Rich first, letting her fingertips trace along his jaw in a lazy, intimate gesture.

Then, as she reached Steve, she paused.

Her eyes flicked to his lap again, lingering on his cock—on its *girth*, its thickness—before meeting his gaze with an expression so wicked it sent a fresh pulse of arousal through him.

"Such a *thick* one," she murmured, her voice dripping with teasing amusement. "*Shorty* might not have the reach... but I *do* love a good stretch."

Steve sucked in a sharp breath as Beth let out a soft, knowing chuckle beside him.

Chloe finally straightened, turning toward Beth with a gleam in her eyes.

"Your turn," she said smoothly.

Steve barely had time to register his own mortification before Beth stepped forward—*and smiled*.

And just like that, his world tilted again.

"Now," Chloe purred, her voice dripping with mischief, "I *think* they both enjoyed the show."

Beth let out a breathy laugh, unable to resist the wicked amusement in Chloe's tone. But her laughter caught in her throat as she glanced down at Steve.

The evidence was *undeniable*.

A thick strand of precum glistened at the tip of his stiff cock, a betraying sheen of arousal catching the dim deck lights. Rich was in a similar state, his long, slightly thinner shaft twitching as his chest rose and fell with anticipation.

Beth swallowed.

She had been naked around others before. She had flirted, danced, teased.

But *this*?

This was something entirely different.

"But first, I think the boys deserve a little relief," Chloe added with a playful smirk.

Without hesitation, she stepped toward Rich's chair, lowering herself gracefully until she was kneeling between his spread legs. She leaned in, her blonde hair cascading over her shoulders, and *without a moment's hesitation*, she pressed a slow, teasing kiss to the swollen head of his cock.

Rich groaned, his fingers curling instinctively against the armrests, even though he couldn't move.

Beth's stomach tightened.

She just did it. Just like that. No hesitation, no embarrassment. Chloe took what she wanted, reveled in the power of it, and clearly *enjoyed* every second of watching Rich squirm.

Beth's pulse pounded as she turned back to Steve. His cock twitched at the sudden attention, the sticky bead of cum still glistening at his tip. He was waiting, his breath uneven, his eyes *locked* onto hers.

She could do this.

Beth licked her lips, nerves clashing with arousal, her hands resting lightly on Steve's thighs as she lowered herself between his legs.

She hesitated, her lips just a breath away from him, her mind racing.

Could she really do this?

But then, from the corner of her eye, she saw Chloe.

Saw the way her tongue flicked out, swirling around the head of Rich's cock with slow, sensual strokes, never taking him fully into her mouth—*just teasing*, just *torturing*.

Rich groaned again, his hips twitching as he tried to push forward, but the restraints held him firm. Chloe giggled, pulling back just slightly, *just* enough to deny him, her lips glistening with his arousal.

It was a *performance*.

And suddenly, Beth understood.

She wasn't just pleasuring Steve—she was *showing off*.

With a deep breath, she leaned in, letting her warm breath fan over Steve's aching tip before she finally pressed her lips against it.

Steve inhaled sharply, his thighs tensing beneath her fingers.

Beth parted her lips slightly, her tongue flicking against the bead of precum, tasting the saltiness as she swirled it away. She let out a small, hesitant moan as she sucked gently on the tip, collecting every bit of his release before swallowing.

Steve's body *jerked*.

She had never done anything like this in front of another person before. And yet, as she pulled back, looking up at Steve's face—his head tilted back, his lips parted, his *entire body tense*—she felt something new.

Power.

Chloe giggled, licking her own lips as she finally slid Rich into her mouth, taking him inch by inch, slow, deliberate, *exquisite*. She moaned around him, letting the vibrations course through his length before she pulled back, her lips still wrapped tightly around the head.

Beth swallowed hard.

Chloe was *good*.

Really good.

She played with Rich's cock like she *loved* it, like she *owned* it. She teased with her tongue, swirling it around the sensitive ridge of the tip, dragging her lips down *just* enough to make him whimper, then pulling away again, never giving him *everything*.

Beth knew she wasn't nearly as practiced.

But she *was* competitive.

She turned back to Steve, her hand wrapping around the base of his cock, feeling the *thickness* of him, heavier than Rich. She took a deep breath, then opened her mouth wider, sliding her lips over him—slow, wet, deliberate.

Steve let out a guttural groan, his hips jerking slightly, *straining* against his restraints.

That reaction sent a jolt of heat through her.

THE CHALLENGE

Encouraged, she pressed forward, taking him deeper, sucking lightly, her tongue tracing the sensitive underside. She wasn't as teasing as Chloe—she wasn't quite sure how to be—but she compensated by moving with determination, by wanting to make Steve's body react just as much as Rich's.

Chloe glanced over, smirking as she noticed Beth getting more into it.

She pulled off Rich's cock with a wet *pop*, licking her lips as she grabbed the bottle of tequila from the table.

Pouring herself another drink, she filled Beth's glass as well, the golden liquid catching the soft glow of the deck lights.

Beth hesitated, wiping her lips with the back of her hand as she reached for her glass.

Chloe clinked their drinks together, smiling.

"Now that I *really* have their attention," she teased, "why don't you show our men what you can do with some music and a stiff pole? *And believe me, the pun is very much intended.*"

Beth gulped down the drink, feeling the warmth flood her veins.

She set the glass down and looked at the two naked men before her—both stiff, bound, watching her with barely contained anticipation.

Steve's cock twitched against his stomach, a fresh bead of arousal forming at the tip. Rich's shaft flexed, aching for more of Chloe's attention.

Beth's confidence grew.

"They can't touch me," she reminded herself, heart pounding. "They can't *do* anything to me. So I'm free to let go."

Her eyes flickered toward Chloe, watching the way she stood confidently, fully in control, completely unbothered by the fact that two bound, naked men were watching her every move.

Beth exhaled.

She was *not* going to be outdone by her younger friend.

Straightening her back, she took a step toward the pole.

"Start the music," Beth commanded, her voice steady despite the hammering of her heart. She took a deep breath, willing herself to let go as she strutted toward the gleaming metal pole, her hips swaying just enough to keep all eyes locked onto her.

The first song pulsed through the speakers with a deep, provocative beat, the kind that made her body respond instinctively. She reached for the pole, gripping the cool metal as she arched her back, letting her ample ass roll slowly, deliberately, in the direction of the two bound men.

Chloe, ever the orchestrator, smirked as she turned up the volume, seamlessly transitioning into *Taking Care of Business*— a song infamous in the strip club scene. The moment the sultry bassline kicked in, Beth *felt* it.

The nerves that had clung to her melted away.

The music consumed her.

She closed her eyes for a moment, letting the rhythm guide her hips as she gripped the pole tighter, her body beginning to flow with the song. The steel was cold against her palm, grounding her, steadying her as she swayed, rolled, and dipped low, every movement dripping with newfound confidence.

Then she turned.

Steve's breath caught.

Beth had never moved like this before.

She hugged the pole between her breasts, tilting her head back as she dragged the smooth surface between the heavy swells, letting the metal tug at the thin fabric of her bra. Her nipples stiffened instantly, barely concealed beneath the flimsy material.

A minute into the song, she opened her eyes, locking onto the two bound men.

She licked her lips.

Steve twitched, his cock throbbing at the sight of his wife openly *performing* for them, not as the shy woman she had been moments ago, but as something else entirely—something *unleashed.*

Beth reached for the buttons of her blouse, undoing them one by one, teasing as she took her time, keeping them waiting. When she finally shrugged it off, letting it slip down her arms and onto the deck, she stood in nothing but a flimsy lace bra, the cups sheer enough that both men could clearly see the darkened color of her nipples straining against the delicate fabric.

Chloe let out a low, appreciative hum, sipping her drink as she watched the transformation unfold.

Beth smirked, glancing at her before turning her attention back to the pole.

She ran her hands down the length of her body, slowly sliding her fingers over her own skin before pressing her chest against the smooth metal. She rose onto her toes, dragging her tits up along the steel, letting the friction send tiny jolts of pleasure through her as she moved in sync with the music.

Steve groaned, shifting in his restraints, his cock pulsing against his stomach.

Rich's breathing had grown heavier, his long, stiff shaft twitching with every subtle movement Beth made.

Their attention fueled her.

Beth pressed her hips against the pole next, rolling her pelvis in short, slow circles, teasing them with every motion. She moved her hands down, gripping her thighs as she ground herself against the steel, rubbing in short, frantic bursts.

Then she stopped.

Her lips parted slightly in frustration. It wasn't *enough*.

Without hesitation, she stepped back, her fingers moving to the zipper of her shorts.

Steve swallowed hard, knowing what was coming but still unprepared for the raw, unfiltered *need* radiating from his wife as she yanked the zipper down and let the shorts fall to her feet.

She kicked them aside, leaving herself in nearly transparent lace panties and the delicate bra.

Steve groaned aloud.

Beth had never exposed herself like this before, *not like this*—not as a performance, not in front of another man.

And she didn't stop there.

She returned to the pole, grinding against it, her panty-covered mound sliding against the steel as she moved her body with increasing urgency. The friction sent shivers through her, and as she tilted her head back, eyes fluttering shut, she *moaned*.

Soft at first. Then louder.

The sound sent shockwaves through Steve's body, his cock twitching so hard he *ached*.

Beth wrapped her arms around the pole, alternately pressing her breasts and her soaked mound against the cool surface, riding it with a sensuality she hadn't even known she possessed.

She *felt* powerful.

Desired.

Completely uninhibited.

And she didn't *care* who was watching anymore.

The song built toward its crescendo, and with a final, deep roll of her hips, Beth slowly slid down the pole, her legs parting as she collapsed onto the floor, sprawled, breathless, utterly spent.

Her chest rose and fell with heavy breaths, her skin flushed, a lazy, satisfied smile curling her lips.

For a moment, everything was *silent*, except for the last fading beats of the music.

Then Chloe exhaled, sipping her drink.

"Well," she murmured, amusement thick in her tone, "someone just *found herself*."

Beth let out a breathy laugh, her head lolling to the side.

Steve, however, couldn't speak.

Neither could Rich.

Because *fuck*.

They had never seen anything *hotter*.

Steve was close enough to see it—the *obvious* wet spot between Beth's open thighs.

A fresh rush of arousal surged through him as he realized that, at some point near the end of her dance, his wife had *climaxed*. Not from being touched, not from anything physical beyond the friction of the pole and her own movements—she had *come* simply from the power, the exposure, the raw thrill of being watched.

His cock throbbed at the thought.

Chloe knelt beside Beth, her touch gentle as she ran her fingers along the inside of her friend's thigh. "That was amazing, Beth," she murmured, her voice rich with admiration. "I think *I* need to take some lessons from *you*."

Beth let out a breathy laugh, still catching her breath, her skin glowing with exertion and something deeper—satisfaction, confidence.

Chloe helped her to her feet, and together they turned toward the two bound men.

Steve felt his pulse quicken as both women surveyed them, standing tall, fully clothed—*in control*—while their husbands lay naked, restrained, their cocks hard and desperate, their bodies betraying the raw sensuality of what they had just witnessed.

Chloe smirked, placing a hand on her hip.

"Do you think we should give our men some *relief*?" she teased, her gaze flicking between them, her grin wicked.

Steve's cock pulsed in response, aching at the mere *suggestion* of what she meant.

His mind raced.

Was this it?

Was this how it finally happened?

Would he finally feel Chloe's warm, tight *tunnel* engulf him?

Would Beth, his *sweet*, beautiful wife, finally feel the weight of another man—Rich—pressing her down, filling her, stretching her in ways Steve *couldn't*?

The thought sent an intoxicating mix of panic and arousal crashing through him. He couldn't move, couldn't *speak*—he could only lie there, restrained, his body utterly at their mercy as the two women approached his lounger.

Chloe stopped just beside him, turning to Beth, her smile coy as she rested a hand on her shoulder.

"Looks like Steve needs some of your *tender, loving care*," she purred. "Why don't you make him happy... while I see what I can do for *my* Rich?"

Steve exhaled slowly, his body shuddering as relief flooded his brain.

Not yet.

Not tonight.

He wouldn't have to watch Rich take Beth—not yet, at least.

But then, why did he feel a *tiny pang of disappointment* nestled within the relief?

His thoughts scattered as Chloe pivoted toward Rich's chair, gliding over to her bound husband with the grace of a predator about to pounce. Steve watched, enthralled, as she knelt between Rich's spread legs, reaching between his thighs with slow, deliberate movements.

Her fingers trailed lightly over his heavy balls, rolling them gently in her palm before dragging her nails *upward* along the sensitive underside of his shaft.

Rich *groaned* loudly, his hips jerking slightly within his restraints, his cock flexing under Chloe's playful torment.

Steve swallowed hard, his own cock twitching in response.

Chloe wasn't just *touching* Rich—she was *toying* with him, *teasing* him, using the sharp edge of her nails to scrape down his length before returning to the base, where she traced lazy circles with her fingertips.

Rich's body trembled.

Steve's mouth went dry.

Chloe *was incredible.*

And now…

Beth was standing beside *him.*

His wife, his beautiful, *newly uninhibited* wife.

She looked down at him, her lips slightly parted, her chest still rising and falling from exertion, her body still *buzzing* from her own climax.

She was about to *touch him*.

To pleasure him.

To *compete* with Chloe in the only way that mattered.

And *fuck*, he was ready for it.

Beth moved with slow, deliberate care as she knelt beside Steve's restrained form, her fingers grazing lightly along his thigh before wrapping around the thick base of his cock. She stroked him gently, her touch slow and exploratory, her fingertips gliding over the velvety skin, tracing the bulging veins as if she were committing every inch of him to memory. The heat of his arousal pulsed against her palm, the weight of him familiar yet strangely new in this setting, under these circumstances.

She met his gaze, her expression soft yet filled with something deeper—*intent*. There was no rush in her movements, no hesitation, just a quiet, simmering awareness between them.

"Did you enjoy my show?" she whispered, her voice lower than usual, carrying a husky, intimate edge. She leaned in just slightly, her breath warming his skin, her lips curving in something between a smirk and an invitation. "I wanted to excite you… and make you proud of me."

Steve let out a shuddering breath, his chest rising and falling unevenly. Her words, her touch, the way she was looking at him —it was all too much, and not enough at the same time.

"Oh, God, yes," he gasped, his voice raw with need. "Beth… I didn't think I could ever get this hard again. Watching you —*fuck*, watching you like that—I couldn't believe you would actually do it."

Beth's grip on him remained firm, but her expression faltered slightly, a flicker of uncertainty crossing her features. Even after all that, after the way she had moved, the way she had claimed the space and owned the moment, there was still a small part of her that questioned.

"Did I show too much?" she asked, almost tentatively.

Steve shook his head immediately, swallowing hard, his Adam's apple bobbing as he fought to keep control of himself. "Beth, no. It's nothing we haven't *seen* before, but the way you *moved*—the way you let go like that—it was... *Jesus*." He exhaled sharply, struggling to find the words. "It was more than sexy. It was *intoxicating*."

Beth let out a slow breath, watching the way his muscles tensed beneath her hands. She hadn't been sure—hadn't *known* if what she had done was too much, if it had changed something between them. But the way he looked at her now, the way his body *reacted* to her, told her everything she needed to know.

"You liked seeing me that way?" she asked softly, her fingers tightening just slightly around his cock.

Steve's response wasn't verbal at first—his body answered before his words could. His length twitched in her grasp, the thick weight of him pulsing as if to confirm what he couldn't yet say. When he did find his voice, it was hoarse, full of unfiltered want.

"*I fucking loved it.*"

The rawness of his confession sent a slow wave of heat through Beth's body, settling deep in her core. She bit her lip, watching the way his cock throbbed, how his hips twitched ever so slightly, restrained but eager. She had spent so much time believing that this part of herself—the part that could *enjoy* being watched, that could embrace being desired—was something she wasn't capable of. But now?

Now she *knew* better.

Shifting slightly, she let her fingers glide up his shaft, her thumb sweeping over the swollen head, spreading the slick bead of precum across his skin. The sound he made—a low, desperate groan—sent a fresh rush of confidence through her.

"Then let me make you feel even better," she whispered, her voice carrying the full weight of her newfound power.

Steve's head fell back against the lounger, a broken moan escaping his lips. His body was completely at her mercy, helpless beneath her touch.

And Beth—his *wife*, his beautiful, *newly awakened* wife—felt nothing but satisfaction as she leaned in, ready to show him just how much she had learned.

Beth kept her fingers moving as they spoke, her grip on Steve's thick shaft slow and deliberate, her other hand trailing featherlight strokes over the sensitive skin of his balls. The contrast between her firm strokes and the teasing flickers of her fingertips had his breath coming in uneven waves, his body straining against the restraints as if aching to reach for her.

"Does that feel good to you?" she asked, her voice sultry but genuinely curious.

Steve let out a shaky chuckle, his fingers flexing against the armrests as he exhaled sharply. "Absolutely. *Obviously,* you can do anything you wish with me in my present condition."

Beth smirked at his playful tone, but there was something *real* behind his words—an unspoken *surrender*. Here he was, bound and exposed, completely at her mercy, and he *liked* it. The thought sent a thrill through her.

"Hey, that's right," she mused, squeezing him just slightly before releasing, letting her fingertips tease their way back up his shaft. "I *can* do whatever I want." She tilted her head, her eyes gleaming with mischief as she let her nails rake ever so lightly against his inner thigh, watching the way he twitched in response.

Steve groaned, his cock flexing in her grasp.

"I think I'll *do more* while I've got you strapped down," she teased, licking her lips before slowly lowering her head.

She let her breath wash over the sensitive tip first, just to see his reaction. His thighs tensed, his chest rising and falling as he *waited*—helpless, anticipating. Then, finally, she parted her lips and *licked*, the tip of her tongue circling the swollen head, collecting the salty droplets that had already formed there.

Steve let out a strangled moan, his hips jerking slightly before the restraints held him firm.

Beth *felt* the power shift in that moment.

She had *never* done this in front of anyone before. She had never had the confidence to simply *take* what she wanted. But now, with Steve bound and aching beneath her, his body reacting to her every flick of the tongue, she felt a rush of heat—*excitement*, pleasure that wasn't just about giving but about *owning* the moment.

She licked him again, slow and deliberate, tracing the ridge of his tip before wrapping her lips around him and sucking gently.

Steve gasped, his head pressing back against the lounger.

Encouraged, Beth took more of him, sliding her mouth down his shaft, letting her tongue press against the thick veins as she went deeper. She wasn't as skilled as Chloe—she *knew* that—but she didn't need to be. The way Steve throbbed in her mouth, the way his body tensed and trembled under her touch, told her everything she needed to know.

This wasn't just for him.

This was *for her*, too.

And she was going to enjoy *every* second of it.

Beth's breath was ragged, her body trembling with anticipation as she looked down at her bound husband. Her lips were parted, her cheeks flushed with arousal, and in that moment, something *shifted* inside her—an acceptance, a *claiming* of this new side of herself that had been unleashed tonight.

"I need you now!" she finally declared, her voice firm, leaving no room for hesitation.

Steve's eyes widened at her sudden decisiveness, his cock throbbing against his stomach as she climbed onto the lounger, straddling him with practiced ease. Her hands trailed over his chest as she settled herself over him, the heat between her legs tantalizingly close to his aching shaft.

With no more teasing, no more restraint, she hooked a finger into the side of her sheer panties and tugged them aside, exposing the glistening pink folds that were already dripping with need. Without ceremony, she lowered herself onto him, letting out a long, desperate moan as his thick cock stretched her open.

Steve groaned in relief, his fingers flexing helplessly against the restraints as Beth took him *all the way in*, sinking down until she was completely filled.

For a long moment, neither of them moved.

They simply *felt*.

The familiar, intoxicating sensation of being connected, of fitting together perfectly, of her walls clenching around him as they adjusted to each other's heat.

Steve's head fell back against the lounger, his breath coming out in shuddering gasps. "Jesus, Beth..."

But Beth wasn't listening. Her attention had been stolen.

Just a few feet away, Chloe was on her knees, her lips wrapped around Rich's cock, taking him deep into her mouth with slow, torturous skill. Rich's head was thrown back, his fingers twitching against his restraints as his chest rose and fell in heavy, erratic breaths.

But it wasn't just the way Chloe worked him with her mouth that caught Beth's attention.

It was the way her free hand was buried between her own legs, fingers gliding through her slick folds, circling her swollen clit as she pleasured herself in time with every movement of her mouth.

Beth swallowed hard, her thighs quivering around Steve's hips.

She knew she *shouldn't* be watching, but she *couldn't* look away.

And that's when Rich's gaze met hers.

Her breath caught.

He wasn't watching *Chloe*.

He was watching *her*.

His blue eyes darkened with something unmistakable—*want*. His stare was heated, focused, and Beth *knew* what he was thinking, what he was imagining. He wanted to be inside her the way Steve was. He wanted to feel her riding *him*.

And what terrified her most?

The way her own body *responded* to that thought.

Her hips started moving instinctively, rolling forward, grinding down against Steve's cock as if responding to Rich's gaze alone.

Steve groaned beneath her, his body arching up as she began to ride him in earnest.

She tried to tear her eyes away from Rich, tried to *focus* on her husband—the man *inside* her, the man she *loved*—but every time she glanced back, Rich was still watching. And that gaze…

It *changed* something inside her.

Maybe it was *knowing* he was thinking about what it would be like to be the one beneath her. Maybe it was the subtle acknowledgment deep inside her that *eventually*, before this weekend was over, she would *give* him that opportunity.

Maybe this was the ultimate *tease*.

Either way, she *wanted* him to watch.

Her pace increased, her thighs tightening as she rode Steve harder, faster, taking him deeper with every thrust. His cock stretched her, filling her in a way that sent fire licking up her spine, her slickness making every movement *effortless* as she rolled her hips with desperate, growing need.

Across from her, Chloe let out a loud, shuddering moan around Rich's cock, her fingers moving frantically between her legs as she chased her own climax.

Beth could *hear* how wet she was, could *see* the way her thighs quivered as she pleasured herself while sucking off her husband.

And then, with a gasping cry, Chloe *came*.

Her body tensed, her fingers pressing deep into her pussy as her orgasm wracked through her, making her *jerk* against Rich's cock.

Beth was *so* close now, her own orgasm hovering just out of reach as she fucked Steve with abandon, sweat dripping down her spine, her breasts bouncing with every thrust.

Then she saw it.

Chloe, still shuddering, pulled off Rich with a slick pop, gripping his length as she stroked him furiously, bringing him to the edge.

Rich let out a strangled groan, his cock pulsing, and then he *came*, thick ropes of cum shooting onto Chloe's waiting tongue.

And Beth watched—*fascinated*—as Chloe smiled, tilting her head slightly, letting Steve and Beth both *see* the creamy load resting on her tongue.

Then, maintaining eye contact, she *swallowed*.

Every. Last. Drop.

Steve's cock *jerked* inside Beth, and she *felt* the sharp, unspoken *jealousy* roll off of him in waves.

Beth's brows furrowed in realization. *She's never swallowed for him.*

That small, wicked smirk from Chloe, the satisfaction in her eyes, *taunted* her.

And suddenly, a surge of *competitiveness* flared to life inside Beth.

Her grip on Steve's chest tightened, her nails digging into his skin as she *snapped* her hips down hard, slamming herself onto him, making him *cry out*.

"*Oh, fuck—* Beth!"

She felt it *then*—the sharp, uncontrollable tensing in his body, the way his cock pulsed violently inside her.

"*Come inside me,*" she whispered, her voice thick with challenge.

Steve let out a ragged groan, his body *convulsing* beneath her, his cock throbbing as he *spilled* deep inside her, filling her with his release. The sensation sent Beth *spiraling* after him, her own orgasm crashing over her like a tidal wave.

She *gasped*, her thighs trembling, her head falling back as pleasure *exploded* inside her, making her ride out every last pulse, every last quivering moment.

It wasn't until the haze began to clear, until her breathing slowed, that she lifted her head and looked at Steve.

His face was still slack with pleasure, his eyes heavy with exhaustion.

Then, slowly, she turned her gaze to Chloe—who was still licking her lips, *watching her*.

A silent challenge passed between them.

And Beth knew.

Next time, she might just have to *swallow*.

THE MOMENT OF TRUTH

After releasing the two men from their restraints, Beth and Chloe shared a knowing look before stepping back, allowing their husbands to gather themselves.

Steve rolled his stiff shoulders, flexing his fingers now that circulation had returned to his limbs. His body still hummed with the aftershocks of his orgasm, and yet, a strange, simmering energy remained between them all. It was there in the way Rich exhaled slowly as he stood, in the way Chloe smoothed her hands down her thighs before stretching her arms overhead, her body still flushed from her own release.

Beth, however, was the most intriguing of all.

She made no move to retrieve her blouse or shorts.

Instead, she remained in just her thin lace panties and sheer bra, lounging comfortably as if she had forgotten—or perhaps *chosen*—to leave herself half-dressed. The delicate lingerie did little to hide her curves, and Steve found himself stealing glances, still processing how uninhibited his wife had become in a matter of hours.

They made their way back inside, the shift from the warm night air to the dimly lit house bringing a moment of grounding normalcy. As if on autopilot, Steve helped Rich mix another round of drinks, the rhythmic clinking of ice against glass the only sound between them at first.

It was *odd*—the way they moved, the way they spoke.

There was a slight nervousness now, an almost forced casualness in their conversation, as if trying to pretend that what had just happened outside *hadn't* happened. But it had.

And it *lingered*.

When they returned to the living room, Beth sat on the couch with a slow, measured grace, her body angled slightly toward Steve, but her posture still open toward Rich and Chloe. The thin lace of her panties was stretched tight across her hips, the bra barely containing her breasts, her nipples still slightly visible through the sheer fabric.

And still—*still*—she made no move to cover herself.

Chloe, on the other hand, had slipped back into her tiny shorts and tube top, but the energy she exuded was still the same—confident, playful, *knowing*. She sipped her drink and let the silence settle for a beat too long before smirking over the rim of her glass.

"Well," she finally said, swirling her wine. "That was *quite* the evening."

Beth's lips twitched, fingers tracing the condensation on her glass. "It was," she agreed, her voice softer, but steady.

Rich chuckled, shaking his head as he took a sip of his whiskey. "Can't say I've ever had a night like that before."

Steve lifted his drink to his lips, swallowing the lingering jealousy that still curled in his stomach. He could still *see* Chloe's satisfied smirk, the way she had so *deliberately* swallowed Rich's release in front of them, the way Beth had *seen* it, had *felt* it.

It hadn't been spoken about—not yet.

But it *hung* between them.

Dinner was late, but when they finally sat down at the table, the tension had softened somewhat, though not completely faded. The normalcy of setting plates, pouring wine, and passing food gave them something to focus on, a return to *routine*—but their bodies still carried the weight of what had just happened.

Beth had finally slipped on a robe before joining them at the table, but it was *thin*—almost an afterthought, a mere suggestion of modesty rather than a true covering. The deep V-neck dipped low, exposing the delicate swell of her breasts, and the loose knot at her waist left enough of a gap that Steve *knew* she was still only in her panties underneath.

And when she crossed her legs beneath the table, the fabric parted just *enough* to keep Rich's gaze flickering downward every so often.

Steve *noticed*.

Beth *noticed him noticing*.

And Steve realized something.

This was *still* a game.

The wine flowed smoothly, and they talked of other things—work, mutual friends, upcoming plans—but the undercurrent of *what they had done* never left the room. It was there in the way Beth's fingers occasionally brushed the stem of her wine glass, her nails tapping lightly as if distracted. It was there in the way Chloe occasionally let out a breathy little laugh, as if remembering something particularly *delicious* from earlier.

And it was there in the way Rich's hand occasionally curled into a fist against the table, his eyes dark with the memory of watching Beth ride Steve—of watching her body move, of seeing her come undone.

By the time dessert was finished, the tension had reached a slow simmer again, no longer forced, no longer nervous—just *there*, waiting, *anticipating.*

Chloe leaned back in her chair, stretching her arms behind her head, arching her back slightly as she looked at Beth with a smirk.

"So," she said, voice lazy, teasing. "What's next?"

Beth took another slow sip of her wine, meeting Chloe's gaze.

And *smirked back.*

"Well, I'd *love* to see you at our club," Chloe gushed, swirling the last of her wine in her glass. Her eyes gleamed with excitement as she turned to Beth. "We have *so* much fun every time we go." She paused for dramatic effect before adding, "But that's not until tomorrow evening. And in the meantime, I've planned a *shopping* trip for tomorrow morning—lunch at the mall, a little girl time."

Beth perked up at the idea, brushing a stray strand of hair behind her ear. "Sounds like fun," she said easily. "I *do* need a few new things to go with my black dress."

Rich groaned, shaking his head before leaning back in his chair. "Count me out," he muttered. "The game starts at noon, and I'm *definitely* sleeping in."

Chloe waved him off with a dismissive smirk. "Oh, you and Steve aren't *even* invited," she informed him, her tone dripping with amusement. "You two will have to entertain yourselves until tomorrow night. Beth and I have *serious* shopping to do."

Beth chuckled softly, sipping her wine. The idea of a day out with Chloe was strangely appealing. There was something about her confidence, her way of moving through the world that made Beth want to follow her lead—just to see where it took her.

With dinner finished, Chloe leaned back and stretched, giving Rich a pointed look. "Alright, babe, you're on cleanup duty."

Rich didn't argue, just sighed dramatically before gathering plates and stacking them with the ease of someone *used* to following orders.

Beth watched with a raised brow before nudging Steve with her foot under the table. "You should help too," she teased, eyes dancing.

Steve groaned but pushed back from the table, grabbing the remaining glassware and silverware, saving Rich another trip.

As the men moved toward the kitchen, Beth leaned in closer to Chloe, lowering her voice. "It's nice how well you have Rich *trained*," she mused, glancing over her shoulder at the two men. "He's *so* much nicer than the last time we were together."

Chloe smirked, swirling the last sip of wine in her glass before bringing it to her lips. "Rich has learned that he enjoys home life a *lot* more when *I'm* in charge," she confided, tilting her head slightly. "You saw for yourself earlier—how *docile* he's become."

Beth nodded, remembering the way Rich had responded to Chloe's touch, her commands. It had been...*fascinating* to watch.

Chloe's smirk deepened as she leaned in slightly, lowering her voice to something silkier, more intimate. "Of course," she added with a low chuckle, "I *make sure* he knows it's *worth* his while."

Beth's stomach tightened at the implication, a fresh rush of curiosity and heat creeping through her veins.

Before she could respond, Steve returned to the table, rubbing his hands together. "Alright," he announced, breaking the moment. "What's for dessert?"

Chloe's grin was immediate and *wicked*. She reached for the nearly empty wine bottle, swirling it absentmindedly before setting it down and lifting a brow at him.

"How about a snifter of Cognac," she purred, "*and* a can of whipped cream to take to bed with you?"

Steve barked out a laugh, but there was heat in his eyes. "Sounds like a winner," he admitted, reaching for his drink. "After *this* evening's show, I'm *definitely* ready for an early bedtime."

Beth felt her cheeks warm slightly, but she didn't protest. She wasn't sure what excited her more—the idea of what *Steve* had in mind…

Or what *Chloe* had just planted in hers.

An hour later, Steve and Beth were stretched out comfortably in the guest room down the hall from Rich and Chloe's master suite. The dim glow of the bedside lamp cast soft shadows across their bodies, the remnants of wine still warm in their veins.

Steve shook the cold can of whipped cream in his large hand, eyeing it with an amused smirk. "Hell, I thought Chloe was *kidding* when she said whipped cream," he mused, the metal cool against his palm.

Beth stretched, her body relaxed yet tingling with anticipation. "Well," she said, arching a brow, "if you're planning on using that on me, you'd better do it *soon*—because I'm *horny*, and you need to *fix that*."

Steve chuckled at her impatience, but the hunger in her voice sent a fresh throb of arousal through him.

Clothes quickly disappeared between them, tossed carelessly to the floor as they stretched out naked on the king-sized bed. Beth reached for the can first, swiping it from the nightstand before Steve could protest. She straddled his lower legs, her bare skin warm against his thighs, her mischievous grin telling him she had already decided how this would go.

"I get to go first," she declared, shaking the can before angling it toward his lap.

Steve opened his mouth to argue, but before he could speak, the cold spray of whipped cream landed on his stiff cock, making him *jump*.

"Jesus, *that's cold!*" he yelped, laughing as he twitched beneath her.

Beth giggled, spreading the foam with her fingers, letting the contrast of cool cream and his burning heat tease her own senses. "You'll survive," she purred, running a slow fingertip up his length before bending forward.

Steve barely had time to prepare before her tongue swept over him, warm and wet against the sugary cream. His stomach tightened as she took her *time*, licking in slow, lazy strokes, cleaning every inch of him with deliberate care.

Globs of cream dripped onto his scrotum, and without hesitation, Beth moved lower, sucking him clean with playful flicks of her tongue, humming in approval as she worked.

"*Oh, man,*" Steve groaned, his head pressing back into the pillows. His fingers curled into the sheets, his thighs tensing beneath her. "*Do that again.*"

Beth pulled back, her lips sticky, her chin smeared with traces of whipped cream. She licked her lips, smirking as she tilted her head. "No, no," she teased, wiping her chin with the back of her hand. "Now *you* have to do *me*."

She rolled onto her back, stretching out with a lazy, satisfied sigh, her legs falling open just enough to make Steve's mouth go dry.

He shook the can, shaking his head with an amused chuckle. "*Fine*," he murmured, leaning over her. "*But I'm going to do this properly.*"

Beth gasped as the first cold puff of cream landed atop her pubic mound, the cool sensation making her thighs twitch. Steve grinned as he continued, drawing a slow, teasing line up her stomach, swirling it around her navel before traveling higher.

He paused to admire his work, then added two *perfect* dollops atop her nipples, watching as they stiffened beneath the weight of the sweet foam.

Beth shivered beneath him, her skin reacting to the contrast of cool cream and the heat of his touch.

"You look *good enough to eat*," Steve murmured, his grin wolfish as he lowered his head.

Beth laughed, wiggling beneath him. "*Then get busy*," she teased, motioning with her fingers for him to begin.

Steve didn't need another invitation. He started at her stomach, dragging his tongue up the sticky trail he'd created, taking his time, savoring her taste. When he reached her breasts, he flicked his tongue over one whipped-cream-covered nipple, then the other, before sucking one into his mouth with slow, agonizing precision.

Beth let out a breathy moan, arching her back. "*Ohhh, Steve...*"

He worked his way downward, devouring the cream, his lips and tongue leaving a glistening path in their wake. By the time he reached her thighs, Beth was *squirming*, her hands fisting in the sheets.

He hovered over her mound, pausing just long enough to hear her *whimper* in frustration before finally dragging his tongue through the sticky cream covering her slit, parting her folds as he *tasted* her beneath the sweetness.

Beth *shuddered*. "Oh, God, Steve—*"

He took his time, licking and teasing, alternating slow, sensual strokes with gentle flicks against her clit. But just as Beth's moans turned into desperate, broken gasps, just as her hips *lifted* to meet his mouth—

He pulled away.

Beth's eyes flew open, her face a mix of confusion and *betrayal*. "*What the fuck?*" she panted.

Steve wiped his chin with the back of his hand, grinning. "*You're impatient,*" he teased, shifting his body up over hers. "*Maybe I should make you wait a little longer.*"

Beth *growled*—an actual *growl*—and grabbed his arms, pulling him *down* over her. "*I need to be fucked,*" she demanded, her voice low, *urgent*. "*Right now.*"

Steve's cock pulsed in response to her raw, unfiltered need.

"*Yes, ma'am,*" he muttered, lining himself up before slamming into her in one deep, fluid thrust.

Beth cried out, arching beneath him, wrapping her legs around his waist as he started to move, setting a *hard, desperate* rhythm.

Steve barely had time to register a single thought beyond how *fucking good* she felt around him, how *incredible* she looked beneath him, writhing, panting, her skin still sticky with the remnants of their playful indulgence.

And somewhere, in the back of his hazy, pleasure-clouded mind, one thought flickered—

I wonder if Rich is doing the same thing to Chloe right now.

The image sent a fresh jolt of arousal through him, and he *drove* into Beth harder, swallowing her moan with his mouth as the whipped cream can rolled forgotten onto the floor.

As Chloe and Rich made their way back to their master suite, she couldn't help but smirk, leaning in close to whisper in his ear.

"See? *Told you* they'd use the whipped cream," she murmured, her voice rich with amusement. "You *men* think you're so unpredictable, but give you a can of sugar and a naked woman, and you're *so* easy to figure out."

Rich chuckled, but his breath was uneven, his arousal undeniable. He had been *hard* from the moment they left the dinner table, and the knowledge that Beth and Steve were just down the hall, *right now*, covered in whipped cream and fucking like animals, only made it worse.

Curiosity gnawed at them both.

They slowed as they neared the guest room, the muffled sounds of Beth's moans and the rhythmic creak of the bed reaching their ears.

Chloe bit her lip, eyes darkening.

"Let's peek," she whispered, barely audible.

Rich hesitated for only a second before following her lead. They moved carefully, pressing their backs against the wall just outside the slightly ajar door. Chloe risked a glance inside, her breath catching at what she saw.

Beth was spread out beneath Steve, her legs wrapped tightly around his waist, her fingers clawing at his back. Steve's body was *tense*, glistening with sweat, his powerful frame moving with deep, *slow* thrusts.

Chloe's gaze dipped lower—and her lips parted slightly in appreciation.

Even coated in the remnants of whipped cream, there was no mistaking it.

Steve's cock was *thick*.

Thicker than Rich's, than most men she'd been with. She could see how Beth stretched around him, how her body clung to every inch of his girthy shaft, and the sight sent a wicked thrill through her veins.

She turned her head slightly, just enough for Rich to hear her breathy whisper.

"Damn," she murmured, her lips curving into a smirk. "I always *suspected* Steve was packing some serious *girth*... but seeing it in action?" She let out a low, amused hum. "*Now* I get why Beth looked so satisfied at dinner."

Rich tensed beside her, his cock twitching against his pants.

Chloe felt it.

And she *loved it*.

Her fingers drifted down, palming the outline of his erection through the fabric. "What's wrong, baby?" she teased, glancing up at him with feigned innocence. "Feeling a little *competitive*?"

Rich growled low in his throat, his hand tightening on her hip.

Chloe giggled, stepping back and tugging him toward their own room. "Come on," she whispered, voice dripping with promise. "I *wanna* play too."

The moment the door clicked shut behind them, she wasted no time.

Dropping to her knees, she tugged his belt open, yanking his pants and briefs down in one swift motion. His cock sprang free, thick and ready, veins pulsing with anticipation.

Chloe reached for the can of whipped cream, shaking it before pointing the nozzle directly at his stiff shaft.

"Let's see if I can make you forget about how thick Steve's cock is," she purred, tilting her head before pressing the cold foam to the tip of his cock.

Rich sucked in a sharp breath as the contrast of cold cream and her warm hand sent shivers up his spine.

Chloe grinned.

And then—*without breaking eye contact*—she *licked.*

Chloe's lips wrapped around Rich's cock, her tongue tracing the thick vein along the underside before she sucked him into her mouth with slow, deliberate ease. She savored the weight of him, the heat, the way his body tensed beneath her touch. The whipped cream had already melted, leaving behind only a faint sweetness that she lazily licked away. She knew exactly what she was doing, taking her time, controlling the pace, making him feel every second of her attention.

Rich groaned, tilting his head back, his fingers gripping the edge of the dresser for support. "Fuck, Chloe..." he breathed, his voice thick with pleasure. His hips twitched slightly, a reflex, but he knew better than to thrust forward. She wouldn't allow it. Not yet.

Chloe smirked around him, flicking her tongue against the sensitive ridge of his tip before pulling back. She ran her tongue up the length of his shaft, teasing, making sure he felt her warm breath before she took him in again. She set the pace, slow and methodical, sucking just hard enough to make him groan, but not enough to push him over the edge. She *wanted* him desperate. She *wanted* him needy. *She* was the one in control.

Across the hall, Beth and Steve lay tangled in bed, their bodies still warm from their own passionate lovemaking. The house was mostly silent now, except for the unmistakable sounds filtering through the thin walls—the wet, obscene rhythm of Chloe's mouth working over Rich's cock, the deep, guttural groans he let out in response.

Beth shifted slightly, pressing her back against Steve's chest as she tilted her head. "I can hear them," she murmured, her voice hushed.

Steve exhaled slowly, rubbing a hand over her hip. "Yeah," he admitted. "It sounds like Rich is getting taken care of."

Beth frowned slightly, her fingers tracing idle patterns over Steve's chest. "I thought Chloe was the dominant one," she mused. "But it seems like she's been sucking his cock all night."

Steve hesitated before responding. "Yeah," he finally said. "Doesn't really fit, does it? If she's in charge, why is she the one always on her knees?"

For a moment, they just listened. Chloe wasn't just performing a service. She *enjoyed* it. The soft hum of satisfaction in her throat, the teasing slowness, the way she let Rich moan and beg—it was obvious she was doing this because she *wanted to*. And she was in complete control of his pleasure.

Beth's fingers stilled against Steve's chest as realization settled over her. "She *is* in charge," she whispered.

Steve tensed slightly beneath her. "What do you mean?" His voice was quiet, thoughtful.

Beth swallowed, her mouth suddenly dry. "She's not doing this *for* him—she's doing it because she *likes it*." She paused, listening to the shift in sounds, the change in rhythm, the way Rich groaned louder before Chloe slowed down again. "She's in control of his pleasure. *She* decides how much he gets, when he gets it. She's teasing him, making him *wait* for it."

Steve was silent, his breathing a little heavier now. Chloe wasn't just pleasuring Rich—she was *toying* with him. Using her mouth to wind him up, to push him toward the edge only to pull away at the last second. She was *holding his orgasm hostage.*

Rich's moans turned desperate. "Ohhh, fuck, Chloe... I'm—*I'm close—*"

Then, suddenly—silence.

Beth blinked, waiting, listening. "Did she... stop?"

Through the wall, Chloe's voice filtered in, teasing, dripping with amusement. "Did you think I was gonna let you finish, baby?"

Rich let out a strangled groan, full of frustration. "Chloe—oh *fuck, please—*"

Beth's body tensed. *She denied him.*

Then the sounds *changed*. No more sucking, no more desperate groans from Rich. Instead, Chloe moaned.

Beth sucked in a sharp breath. "Oh my God," she whispered. "She's making him eat her out now."

Steve's fingers flexed against her waist as they listened, as Chloe let out a long, drawn-out sigh of pleasure. She was *taking* her own pleasure now, moaning, gasping, guiding Rich as he worked between her legs. She wasn't just lying there—she was *directing* him, sighing commands, making him *earn* the right to please her.

Her moans grew louder, her pleasure mounting, her voice sharp with need. "Mmm, just like that... deeper, baby... *ohhh, fuck, yes*—"

Beth felt heat crawl up her spine. Chloe had been teasing Rich for *so long*, edging him, making him think he was about to come, only to *deny* him. And now? Now she was taking *everything* for herself, reveling in it.

Minutes passed, and then Chloe cried out, her orgasm rolling through her, gasping as she rode out every last pulse of pleasure. Then—silence.

Beth's heartbeat pounded in her ears as she waited, and then she heard it.

Rich's voice, low and wrecked. "Please, Chloe," he whispered. "Please let me come..."

Beth's stomach twisted. *He's begging her.*

Chloe let out a soft, satisfied hum, followed by a wicked laugh. "Oh, baby," she cooed. "You were lucky to come earlier. Now, go to sleep—you've got a *big* day ahead of you."

A groan from Rich. A deep sigh. Then nothing.

Beth exhaled shakily, staring up at the ceiling. Chloe had denied him. *Easily.* Without hesitation. As if it wasn't even a question. And she had *loved* it.

Beth's fingers curled into the sheets. She had *never* thought about control like that before—never imagined teasing Steve, making him *beg, holding him there* at the edge while she took what *she* wanted first.

And yet…

Lying there, her body still tingling from their own earlier passion, her mind refused to let the thought go.

Chloe had *absolute power* over Rich. And for the first time, Beth wondered what that kind of control might feel like.

She didn't say a word.

Neither did Steve.

But both of them knew—something had changed between them tonight. And there was no going back.

THE INSTRUCTION

Chloe had left strict instructions for Rich before she and Beth departed for their shopping trip. He was to have snacks and drinks ready by 5:30. She made it clear that they would be thirsty when they returned and that she expected him to be prepared. In exchange, she granted him the luxury of watching sports during the day—a small concession, but one she had emphasized with a playful smirk before kissing him on the cheek and slipping out the door with Beth.

Now, with the house empty except for the two men, Steve and Rich made their way to the den, settling into the plush chairs. Rich grabbed the remote, flicking through the channels before settling on a game. Steve took a sip of his beer, stretching his legs out as he glanced over.

"So," he started casually, "tell me about this club we're visiting tonight."

Rich hesitated for half a second, just long enough for Steve to *notice*. Then, with a small shrug, he took a sip of his drink before answering. "Well, it's... sort of a nightclub," he said, choosing his words carefully. "Music, dancing, a good DJ. There's a big dance floor on the first floor, a solid bar, plenty of tables scattered around. Pretty much your standard club scene."

Steve raised an eyebrow, waiting. Rich was being deliberately vague.

Rich exhaled and continued. "There's also a huge hot tub out back. It's enclosed—kind of an open-air patio feel but private. The upstairs level is a little different, though." He took another sip of his drink, his eyes flickering toward Steve as if gauging his reaction. "Another bar. Some public rooms. Some private rooms. You never really know what you're going to find on any given night."

Steve let the words hang between them for a moment, letting them settle. He took another slow sip of his beer before speaking. "Sounds like a swinger's club to me," he mused, watching Rich's expression. "If the upstairs rooms are what I *think* they are."

Rich chuckled, shaking his head. "People can do whatever they like at the club," he replied smoothly. "You can go, dance, have a few drinks, and never step foot upstairs. Plenty of people do." He paused, then gave Steve a knowing look. "But... you *might* find the whole experience *quite* memorable."

Steve let out a dry laugh, but there was an undeniable flicker of curiosity in his chest. He wasn't *unfamiliar* with the concept, but the idea of *actually being inside* a place like that? Where people were *doing* things, *watching* things, *inviting* others to join? It was something else entirely.

Rich leaned back, his smirk deepening. "You're intrigued, aren't you?"

Steve exhaled, shaking his head slightly. "I think *Beth* is the one I should be asking that question."

Rich shrugged. "Maybe. But from what I *saw* last night, I'd say she's more open-minded than you think." He took another sip, letting the implication settle between them. "The question is... *are you?*"

Steve didn't answer right away. Instead, he let the silence stretch, the weight of the night ahead pressing down on him in ways he hadn't quite expected.

And for the first time, he wondered if *he* was ready for whatever *might* happen next.

Steve swirled the last of his beer in his glass, thinking over Rich's words. The truth was, he was still wrapping his head around everything that had happened last night.

"Beth sure surprised me," he admitted, shaking his head slightly. "I think Chloe might have told her something about the club earlier when they were planning our visit. She's usually pretty conservative—you might even say *private*. But last night…" He exhaled, rubbing a hand over his jaw. "When she had me under her complete control, when she was *riding* me—she just… let go."

Rich chuckled, taking another sip of his drink. "Yeah," he said, his smirk deepening. "That was something to *watch*." He stretched out, rolling his shoulders before adding, "I'll admit, I kept wishing it was *me* under her."

Steve's head snapped up, but Rich didn't look the least bit guilty about the admission. If anything, he looked *amused*.

"She *knew* it too," Rich continued, tapping a finger against the rim of his glass. "She was looking *right* into my eyes most of the time."

Steve swallowed, shifting in his seat as something unfamiliar twisted in his gut. He *hadn't* realized that. Hadn't known that while Beth was lost in her pleasure, she had been *holding* Rich's gaze. The thought sent a strange mix of emotions through him—pride, intrigue… and something darker.

"I didn't know that," he muttered, more to himself than to Rich.

It was *true*—Beth had *changed* last night. He had seen glimpses of a side of her he'd never even known existed. She had *owned* her pleasure in a way she never had before, had *taken* him in front of their friends without an ounce of hesitation. It was raw, uninhibited, *new*.

And the way Rich was looking at him now, like he *knew* Steve was just barely catching up to what had happened, made him feel even more off balance.

Rich chuckled, leaning forward slightly. "I sure hope so, buddy. The club provides the *right* atmosphere for a *private* woman to *blossom*." He swirled his drink, his tone casual—but there was *something* else behind his words. "I'm *sure* you'll enjoy yourself." He paused, then grinned. "Chloe said she was going to make sure you have fun, Steve."

Steve exhaled, his grip tightening slightly around his glass.

Fun.

A word that had suddenly taken on a *whole new meaning*.

The men spent the afternoon watching ball games, their conversation drifting easily between plays, work, and the night ahead. Occasionally, Steve would catch Rich glancing toward the clock, clearly keeping track of when Chloe and Beth would return.

When it neared 5:30, they set aside their drinks and got to work preparing snacks and setting up the bar, following the *instructions* Chloe had given them earlier that morning. Steve found it amusing how naturally Rich followed her directives, and even more amusing how he himself had gone along without question. He had expected the trip to be full of surprises, but what intrigued him most was *his own* willingness to fall into step with the dynamics unfolding around him.

Just as they finished setting the last glasses on the bar, they heard the front door open. Chloe and Beth breezed in, arms full of shopping bags, their laughter filling the house as they carried their purchases toward the bedrooms. Neither woman stopped to offer explanations; they simply disappeared down the hallway, their excited whispers trailing behind them. Steve exchanged a glance with Rich, who only smirked and took another sip of his drink.

A few minutes later, the four of them settled into the den, drinks in hand, sharing stories from the afternoon. Chloe and Beth recounted their shopping trip in playful detail—the absurdly expensive shoes they tried on, the *oh-so-revealing* dresses they debated over, and the men they caught sneaking glances as they moved from store to store. The lighthearted conversation helped dissolve any lingering tension from the night before, making it easier for everyone to slip into the *comfort* of the evening ahead.

But as the clock inched closer to the time they needed to leave, the energy shifted. The reality of *where* they were going—what kind of club this was—settled over them.

Chloe was the first to return, stepping out of the bedroom in a *devastating* red satin dress that clung to every curve, the silky fabric sliding over her body as she moved. It left *just enough* to the imagination while making it abundantly clear that she wore *nothing* beneath it.

Rich let out an appreciative whistle as he rose from his seat, his hands immediately finding her hips. "Damn, babe," he murmured, sliding one hand down to cup her backside through the thin dress. "You're going to turn *a lot* of heads tonight."

Steve nodded in agreement, his eyes flickering over the way the fabric molded to her. "That dress is *dangerous*," he said with a smirk, taking a sip of his drink.

Chloe only smiled, her confidence effortless. "That's the *idea*," she teased, running a hand along Rich's chest before turning toward the hallway. "I better go check on Beth. She's taking longer than expected."

The two men exchanged a glance, hearing the sound of muffled conversation, then a burst of giggling from the guest room. Steve arched an eyebrow.

"Chloe's getting in her head," Rich said with a knowing grin. "Just wait."

A few moments later, Beth finally emerged, her movements hesitant at first, but growing more assured as she stepped into the room.

Steve's breath *caught*.

She wore the sleek black sheath dress with delicate spaghetti straps, the fabric skimming her curves like a second skin. But what made his pulse *jump* was the realization that she was *braless*—her bare nipples pressing subtly but undeniably against the fabric. The way the material draped over her, the way she *moved*, made her feel almost *dangerously* exposed.

Beth lifted her drink and took a sip before meeting Steve's gaze. "Chloe talked me into it," she confessed before he could even ask. "I feel kind of *strange* having my boobs so loose under this little slip of a dress, but... I guess it won't hurt just for tonight."

Steve exhaled slowly, his fingers tightening slightly around his glass. *Christ.* This was *not* the Beth he had arrived with yesterday.

His *wife*—who just days ago had been the picture of quiet modesty—was now standing in front of him, nipples clearly visible beneath her dress, looking both *nervous* and *thrillingly aroused* by her own audacity.

He wondered briefly if Chloe had convinced her to leave her *panties* behind as well.

Rich was clearly wondering the same thing.

The other man sauntered over, his movements easy, confident. He slid an arm around Chloe's waist, kissing her cheek before turning toward Beth with a familiar grin. Without hesitation, he stepped in and placed a quick kiss on Beth's cheek as well, his other hand settling at the small of her back. It was an innocent enough gesture, but Steve's breath *hitched* as he watched Rich's fingers brush *just low enough* to test his suspicion.

Rich pulled back just slightly, and for the briefest moment, Steve *saw* it—the flicker of amusement in Rich's eyes, the slight upturn of his lips.

He had *found* something.

Beth, unaware—or maybe not—took another sip of her drink, her cheeks slightly flushed.

Rich gave Steve a slow, knowing smile before stepping back. "Damn," he murmured. "I was *hoping* you were going full commando, Beth, but I guess we'll just have to settle for a *tiny thong* instead."

Steve's stomach clenched.

Beth *laughed*.

Not nervously, not embarrassed—*but with a playful confidence* that made Steve's cock twitch.

"Well," she said, glancing at Chloe, who was smirking at her like a proud mentor, "Chloe did say tonight was all about... *having fun*."

Rich chuckled, shaking his head as he reached for his drink. "I like this new Beth."

Steve wasn't sure what surprised him more—his *own* reaction to all of this, or the fact that his *wife*—his *sweet, reserved wife*—was actually enjoying it.

Rich clapped him on the shoulder. "Come on, man. Let's finish our drinks and get going. Tonight's just getting started."

Steve swallowed hard, nodding as he took a sip of whiskey.

Something told him this night was about to take them *all* somewhere they hadn't quite expected.

And he wasn't sure if that terrified him… or turned him on.

THE HOST'S DUTIES

Chloe took a slow sip of her drink before setting it down with a playful smirk. She turned her gaze toward Rich, arching a brow. "Rich, you should ask Beth to dance. You're forgetting your duties as host."

Beth lifted her glass, raising it toward her lips, but her eyes flicked toward Steve as she waited for his reaction. Chloe, of course, *added* the question as an afterthought. "You don't mind, do you, Steve?"

Steve exhaled, feeling the whiskey warm in his stomach. "Not at all," he said, meeting Beth's eyes before looking at Rich. "Go ahead."

Rich grinned, already rising from his seat. "Beth?"

Beth hesitated for only a moment, then took Rich's outstretched hand and let him lead her toward the dance floor.

Steve *watched* them go, watched the way Beth's hips swayed beneath the slinky black dress, watched the way Rich's hand settled easily at the small of her back. His stomach tightened —not with jealousy exactly, but something *else*, something he wasn't sure he wanted to name yet.

Chloe's fingers brushed against his wrist, drawing his attention back to her. "I think I owe you some dances anyway," he murmured, reaching for her hand.

Chloe's smirk deepened. "That's right, *you do.*"

She let him lead her onto the dance floor, moving easily against him as the sultry beat of the music wrapped around them.

After several songs, the couples returned to their table, a fresh round of drinks waiting for them. The air between them felt different now—charged in a way that hadn't been there before. The dancing had loosened everyone up, and the alcohol only amplified that effect.

Beth took a sip of her cocktail, eyes sparkling with amusement as she leaned toward Chloe. "Did you *see* that redhead?" she asked, voice lowered slightly. "The top of her dress was down around her waist, and the tall guy she was dancing with was just —*holding* both boobs! Right there in the middle of the floor!"

Chloe laughed, setting down her drink. "Yeah, we've seen her here before," she said, shaking her head. "But not with *that* guy. She's certainly *proud* of her perky white titties." She leaned in slightly. "I think her *real* man must be upstairs right now."

Beth's brows lifted, curiosity flickering across her face. She hesitated for only a moment before tilting her head. "I've been meaning to ask… *what* exactly is upstairs?"

Chloe's lips curved into a knowing smile. "Oh, *upstairs,*" she mused, drawing out the word. "Well, we usually go up there to rest after we're done dancing."

Steve, catching on, leaned in. "I think we should *stroll* up there and see for ourselves, Beth." His voice was casual, but there was something underneath it—something that made Beth's pulse quicken.

Beth swirled the ice in her glass, glancing between Steve and Chloe before locking eyes with Rich. She took a breath, then lifted her chin slightly. "Only if Chloe and Rich come with us," she said, her voice steady. "They *know* their way around. We don't."

Chloe let out a delighted laugh. "Now *that*," she said, standing and smoothing her red satin dress, "is an excellent idea."

Rich drained the last of his drink and smirked. "I think you'll both find it *very* interesting."

Beth shot Steve a quick look, her pulse racing. He reached for her hand, giving it a small squeeze. She squeezed back.

Then, together, the four of them made their way toward the stairs.

Beth's breath caught in her throat as she peered through the one-way mirror into the dimly lit public room beyond. Her fingers instinctively tightened around Steve's forearm, her eyes darting between the scenes unfolding in front of her.

Four couples were scattered around a large, plush pallet in the center of the room, their bodies intertwined in various stages of indulgence. On one side, two pairs were engaged in slow, deliberate acts of oral pleasure—one woman lay back, her thighs spread wide, her lover's head buried between them, while beside them, another man knelt with his face pressed between his partner's legs, gripping her hips as she moaned softly.

To the left, a naked woman was on her hands and knees, her back arched as a man gripped her hips and *thrust* into her, slow and deep. The dim lighting cast shadows over their moving bodies, emphasizing the raw, primal rhythm between them. Across the room, another couple had taken their time, fingers exploring, lips trailing, their clothing slowly coming undone in anticipation of what was to come.

Beth's heartbeat pounded in her ears. *Jesus Christ.* She had *known* what to expect—Chloe had been open about the club's nature—but actually *seeing* it was something else entirely.

Steve's large hands settled firmly on her hips, steadying her. He felt the way her body swayed slightly, the tension humming through her frame. For a split second, he worried she might *faint*—but then, as if seeking his strength, she leaned back against him, pressing her warmth against his chest.

A quiet growl rumbled in his throat as his fingers drifted up, cupping the soft weight of her braless breasts through her thin black dress. The rapid rise and fall of her chest beneath his hands told him everything—she was overwhelmed, but she wasn't recoiling.

She was *reacting*.

Beside them, Chloe exhaled, tilting her head as she took in the erotic display beyond the glass. "Watching them gives me *shivers*," she murmured, her voice rich with intrigue.

Behind her, Rich stepped in, molding his body to hers, pressing his growing arousal between the firm roundness of her ass. His hands slid around her waist, his fingers splaying over her stomach, holding her close as he whispered, "Do you want to *join* them... or keep looking?"

Chloe didn't answer immediately. Instead, she turned her head, locking eyes with Beth, her lips curving into a knowing smile.

"What about you?" she asked, her voice teasing but genuine. "Want to join them? Or move on?"

Beth swallowed hard. Her entire body felt electrified, pulsing with adrenaline, heat, *something* she couldn't quite name yet.

"You mean... *there's more?*" she breathed, her voice barely above a whisper.

Chloe giggled, her amusement warm and knowing. "Oh, sweetheart, *this* is just one of the public rooms. There's another… and several private rooms down the hall."

Beth exhaled, shifting slightly in Steve's grip. Her nerves were still humming, her senses on high alert, but there was no denying the pull of *curiosity* that had taken root inside her.

"Yeah," she said quickly, voice a little breathless. "Let's move on. I need to… *calm down a little.*"

Chloe chuckled, reaching for Rich's hand before glancing back at Steve and Beth. "Come on then," she said, leading the way. "Let's see what else we can find."

As they stepped away from the window, Steve couldn't help but smirk against Beth's ear. "You're not as *shocked* as I thought you'd be," he murmured, his fingers still idly tracing circles over her hips.

Beth bit her lip, a small, nervous smile forming as she glanced up at him. "I don't know what's more shocking," she admitted. "What we just *saw*… or the fact that I didn't *hate* watching it."

Steve's grip tightened slightly, his body reacting to her words in ways he hadn't quite anticipated.

Chloe took Beth's hand, her fingers warm and firm as she guided her a few steps down the dimly lit hallway. The hushed atmosphere of the club seemed to vibrate around them, the distant murmur of voices, the occasional moan slipping through cracks in the doors. The air was thick with something *heady*— a mix of sensuality and anticipation that wrapped around them like a seductive spell.

Beth's pulse quickened as they reached another open doorway. The four of them stepped inside a darkened viewing area, another one-way mirror separating them from the scene beyond.

New sights greeted them.

In the center of the softly lit room, two couples were entwined on a thick pad, their bodies a tangle of pleasure. A striking red-haired woman was on her hands and knees, her toned frame arching beautifully as a younger man knelt behind her. His hands gripped her hips, guiding his long, thick cock in and out of her slick folds with slow, deliberate thrusts. They were angled sideways to the mirror, allowing an *unobstructed* view of every intimate movement—the way his shaft glistened as he withdrew, the way her body rocked in response, the deep sighs of pleasure that escaped her lips.

But there was more.

Beneath the redhead, another woman lay on her back, her face buried in the neatly trimmed ginger bush that was visible between the redhead's parted thighs. She licked hungrily at the point where the man's cock disappeared into her, moaning against her skin, her fingers gripping the redhead's thighs as she pleasured her.

Beth's breath hitched. *She's tasting her while she's getting fucked...*

But the scene didn't end there.

Just beyond them, an older man with streaks of gray in his hair lay flat on his stomach, his hands gripping the thighs of the second woman as he buried his face in her bald, glistening mound. His tongue worked her mercilessly, his shoulders flexing with each movement, lost in his own hunger.

Beth's fingers tightened in Chloe's grasp. "*Oh my God,*" she gasped, her voice barely above a whisper. "They're all *doing* each other at the same time, and that woman is *tasting* her..."

Steve, standing behind her, wrapped an arm around her waist, pulling her against his chest. His voice was low, almost *awed* as he spoke. "I think they've *switched* too," he murmured. His hands traced Beth's stomach through her dress, feeling the tension coiling beneath her skin. "The older guy is *eating* the young gal like crazy."

Beth's stomach clenched, her thighs pressing together. The sight before her was *so raw, so uninhibited.* She had never watched something like this unfold in real time. The *heat* of it, the *intimacy*—the way they all *seemed to lose themselves* in each other's bodies—was something she hadn't expected to *affect* her so deeply.

Her thoughts shattered as the younger man let out a deep, ragged moan, his grip on the redhead's hips tightening. He *slammed* into her with a final thrust, his body going taut.

Beth *saw* it—the subtle jerk of his hips, the tension in his thighs. She *knew* what had just happened.

"There's a condom full," Rich chuckled, his tone thick with amusement.

Beth barely registered the words, her attention locked on what happened next.

The older man, the redhead's presumed husband, moved behind her, his cock already hard again as he slid into the *messy* heat left behind. His movements were different from the younger man's —possessive, almost *territorial* as he took his wife in front of their shared lovers. Meanwhile, the younger man, now spent but not finished, pulled off the condom and let the other woman take his slick, still-throbbing cock into her mouth.

She sucked him greedily, her lips stretched around him, her hands guiding his shaft deeper as she *tasted* everything that had just happened between them.

Beth swallowed hard. Her breathing had turned shallow, her skin *prickling* with something she didn't quite know how to handle.

She wasn't the only one.

Her eyes flicked to Chloe, who stood beside her, her red satin dress *barely* covering her thighs. Her hand was beneath the fabric, the subtle movement unmistakable. She was *touching herself* as she watched, lost in the *frenzy* before her.

Beth's stomach tightened again.

How is she so comfortable doing that… right in front of us?

But more than that…

Why do I feel like I want to do the same?

Beth's fingers twitched at her sides, her body pulsing with a need she hadn't felt before. It was impossible not to react, impossible not to let herself *feel* everything happening in this moment.

She leaned back against Steve's chest again, pressing *just* a little closer.

Steve *felt* it.

His breath hitched against her ear, his hands tightening around her hips.

Beth exhaled slowly, her gaze lingering on the writhing bodies before her. "They're… incredibly brave," she murmured, barely realizing she had spoken out loud. "They must know that others are free to come in and watch them, but they don't care."

Rich chuckled beside her, his voice laced with something *suggestive*. "We could *join* them if you like," he offered smoothly. "You might find that you're brave too, Beth."

Beth's stomach *dropped*, heat flashing through her body in a dizzying wave. "Oh no," she blurted, shaking her head before she could even process the suggestion. "I could *never* do something like that."

It was dark enough that no one could see the deep flush creeping up her cheeks, but Steve *felt* it. His arms were still around her, his fingers resting on her hips, and he didn't miss the subtle *shiver* that ran through her body at the thought.

Rich didn't press the issue, but his smirk told her he'd noticed her reaction.

Steve, ever the instigator, leaned in close, his breath warm against her ear. "Well, you *did* put on a pretty sexy show last night," he reminded her, his voice low, teasing. "And that was before we even got to the bedroom."

Beth swallowed, her pulse quickening. "Yeah, but that was just *the four of us*," she argued, still flustered. "And I was... *pretty tipsy* at the time."

Chloe, sensing Beth's overwhelmed state, came to her rescue. "Would you be more comfortable downstairs, Beth?" she asked, ever the effortless guide in this new world. "I think the dance contest will be starting soon, and that might be more *your* kind of fun."

Steve felt his hopes sink slightly as Beth nodded quickly. "Uh-huh. I think I've seen *enough* up here," she admitted, her voice tinged with nervous excitement. "Let's go back downstairs, okay?"

Chloe winked. "Alright, back to the real world we go."

As they made their way back down to the main floor, the pulsing beat of the music wrapped around them once again, a stark contrast to the hushed, voyeuristic intensity of the upstairs rooms. Steve and Rich grabbed a fresh round of drinks, and soon the four of them were settled at a table toward the edge of the dance floor, the tension from upstairs melting into the lively atmosphere of the club.

Beth sipped her cocktail, still trying to steady her thoughts. The dampness of her tiny thong was a *constant* reminder of what they had just witnessed, of how deeply it had affected her—more than she wanted to admit.

Chloe's voice snapped her back to the present. "There's the *famous* gold pole," she said, nodding toward a sleek, golden firehouse pole near the edge of the dance floor.

Steve followed her gaze, his curiosity piqued. "What happens there?" he asked.

Rich smirked. "Each night, they hold a contest for the sexiest dancer," he explained, leaning back in his chair. "Actually, Chloe *won* one night by doing a version of the dance you saw yesterday. It was *hot as hell* watching her wiggle that sweet little ass for the crowd."

Chloe giggled, swirling her drink. "I think I'll try my luck again tonight if I get the chance," she admitted, her eyes gleaming with mischief. "It's *fun* teasing all the men... and some of the *women* too."

Beth felt her face heat again. *God, how does she do that?* Chloe was so *effortless* in her confidence, her ability to tease and play without hesitation. It was something Beth had never truly considered for herself.

Until now.

Rich turned to Beth, grinning. "You should enter too."

Beth nearly *choked* on her drink.

"What?" she sputtered, her wide eyes darting to Rich, then to Steve, who—of course—*looked entirely too interested* in the idea.

Rich leaned closer, his gaze warm but filled with *knowing*. "From what I *witnessed* last night, you'd have a good shot at winning."

Steve, emboldened by the night, nodded in agreement. "Yeah, you *owned* that pole last night. I'd *love* to see you try your luck." His voice carried something deeper than encouragement—something that sent another *pulse* of heat through her body.

Beth's fingers tightened around the stem of her glass. She was still *reeling* from the sights upstairs, still battling the undeniable arousal swirling in her veins.

Would I even be able to do that? In front of a room full of people?

Her mind *screamed* that it was ridiculous, but her body—still warm, still *buzzing*—wasn't quite so convinced.

She exhaled, shaking her head playfully as she reached out and *poked* Steve in the ribs. "Be careful what you wish for," she teased.

The announcer took center stage, his voice booming over the lively crowd. "Are all you *hot* women ready to *strut your stuff*?" he called out, drawing a chorus of catcalls, whistles, and giggles from the audience. The energy in the club shifted, thick with excitement and anticipation.

The DJ wasted no time, launching into a slow, *sultry* beat that pulsed through the air like a promise. One by one, women started leaving their seats, forming a loose line near the edge of the floor, waiting for their turn to show off.

Chloe stood gracefully, tossing her hair over one shoulder before flashing Rich a playful smile. "Wish me luck, honey," she purred.

Rich grinned, reaching up to cup her ass through the clingy red satin of her dress, giving it a possessive squeeze. "Knock 'em dead," he murmured, his voice laced with both pride and arousal.

Beth watched as Chloe strode toward the growing line of contestants, her movements confident, fluid—*unapologetic*. She exuded an effortless sensuality, one that had nothing to do with what she was *wearing* and everything to do with *how* she carried herself.

For a few minutes, Beth remained still, sipping her drink as she observed the other women. Some twirled lazily around the floor, tossing their hair and shimmying halfheartedly to the beat. A few attempted to use the golden pole, but their movements were stilted, hesitant, lacking the kind of *fluidity* that made a dance truly *seductive*.

Then came the *flashing*.

Two women bared their breasts as their routines ended, grinning wickedly as the crowd cheered. Encouraged by their reception, a curvy blonde stepped forward, a sly grin playing on her lips. She made a dramatic show of twirling in place before turning her back to the audience. With a slow, teasing motion, she lifted her dress up and over her hips, revealing a *bare*, round ass and the hint of her *untrimmed* mound beneath.

The crowd gave a few appreciative hollers, but it wasn't the *reaction* she had been hoping for. Her movements had been too forced, too deliberate—sexy, perhaps, but not *electrifying*.

Beth smirked, shaking her head. "*I could do a lot better than that,*" she murmured under her breath, mostly to herself.

Steve, always *in tune* with her, *heard* her. He turned his head toward her, his dark eyes sparking with something between amusement and challenge. "Then *why don't you?*"

Beth blinked, suddenly aware of how *easily* the words had slipped out. Her heart *skipped*, her pulse suddenly thrumming in her ears.

Steve leaned in closer, his fingers brushing over her knee. "*Loosen up*, babe," he coaxed. "Give Chloe a run for her money."

Beth's stomach *tightened*. The idea of it sent a rush of *heat* through her body—equal parts *fear* and *excitement*.

Her eyes flicked toward the dance floor. Chloe was at the end of the line, watching the other women with a knowing smirk, her body swaying subtly to the music as she waited for her turn.

Could Beth *really* do this?

Her chest rose and fell, her tiny thong *already* a reminder of the arousal she hadn't quite shaken since *upstairs*.

She turned back to Steve, her voice barely above a breath. "You *must* not get angry if I do."

Steve's grin was *instant*, his hand tightening slightly on her knee. "Don't worry, babe," he murmured, his voice low, *entirely too tempting*. "I think you could *win* their little contest." He leaned in, pressing a soft kiss to her ear before whispering, "I *won't* be angry... but I *might* be very, very *proud*."

Beth's breath *hitched*.

His words sent a sharp *thrill* through her, making her skin tingle, her thighs press instinctively together.

Steve pulled back just enough to meet her gaze, his smirk full of knowing. "You only go around *once*, you know."

Beth *exhaled*.

"I'm *going to do it!*" Beth declared, her voice firmer than she expected.

She stood abruptly, crossing her arms over her ample bosom as if steadying herself, but there was no hiding the rush of adrenaline coursing through her.

Rich grinned, exchanging a look with Steve, who was already sitting back in his chair, watching his wife with open curiosity and growing anticipation.

Chloe gave a delighted laugh, swirling what was left of her drink before setting it down. "Good girl," she murmured approvingly.

But before Beth's turn, it was *Chloe's* moment to take the floor.

The DJ cued up a slow, sensual beat, and Chloe wasted no time sliding into the rhythm, moving fluidly across the dance floor with effortless confidence. She twirled, wiggling her hips in slow, deliberate motions, teasing the audience with every step. The room's dim lighting caught the sheen of her red satin dress as it clung to her curves, shimmering with each movement.

When she reached the peak of her routine, she flirted shamelessly with the crowd, lifting the hem of her dress to reveal her long, toned legs. Then, in a well-practiced move, she dipped into a deep squat, her thighs spread just enough for those seated in front to catch a tantalizing glimpse of her tiny lace panties.

The reaction was immediate—cheers, whistles, and playful shouts urging her to *show more.*

Beth felt a jolt of nervous excitement in her stomach. Chloe was completely *in control* of the room, of every gaze locked on her, and she *loved* it.

The song ended, and Chloe gracefully straightened, taking

a quick bow before sauntering back toward their table. She plucked up her drink and took a long, satisfied swallow before flashing a wicked smile at the men. "That was *fun*," she announced, licking a drop of liquor from her lips. "I think I did pretty damn good."

Rich laughed, wrapping an arm around her waist. "Babe, you *owned* that floor."

Steve nodded, still grinning. "Hell yeah, you did."

Before either man could say more, the music shifted, and Beth *moved*.

The low, pulsing beat wrapped around her as she stepped onto the floor, her heartbeat hammering against her ribs. She was *aware* of the expectant hush that settled over the crowd. They had just watched Chloe put on a show—and now, they were waiting to see if *she* could match it.

The first few beats of the song guided her into motion. Beth closed her eyes for half a second, *feeling* the music, letting it seep into her bones before she lifted her arms, running her fingers through her hair and down her neck, drawing attention to the smooth lines of her body.

The sleek black dress hugged her curves as she swayed, her hips moving in slow, tantalizing rolls, her hands skimming down the fabric as if mapping out every inch of her own form.

A murmur rippled through the room.

Encouraged, Beth *let go*.

She turned her back to the audience, arching slightly as she let her hands drift over her body, drawing every eye exactly where she wanted them. The subtle bounce of her breasts beneath the thin fabric. The way the hem of her dress *shifted* just enough to hint at the curve of her ass.

Then she remembered the *pole*.

She turned, her pulse spiking as she moved toward it. The cool metal met her fingertips, sending a shiver up her spine.

It *grounded* her.

Gave her *something to hold on to.*

Beth let the pole become an extension of herself, gripping it as she leaned away, arching her back, her body curving in a way that made her dress shimmer with movement.

The energy in the room *changed*.

The air thickened.

The men watching leaned forward.

Beth felt it.

And she *liked it*.

Her body moved instinctively, fueled by a newfound boldness she hadn't realized she possessed. She *spun*, letting the pole guide her in a slow turn, then pressed against it, letting it slide between her breasts as she dragged herself upward, her head tilting back in something *dangerously close to surrender*.

More cheers.

More *attention*.

Beth's breath came faster, her skin hot beneath the dim lights, her body *thrumming* with something unfamiliar but completely intoxicating.

She wasn't just *dancing*.

She was *performing*.

For Steve.

For Rich.

For herself.

And she wasn't sure she ever wanted to stop.

The club had come *alive* around her. The rhythmic pulse of the music filled the air, merging with the cheers and whistles of an eager audience. Beth felt their energy, their excitement wrapping around her like a force she couldn't ignore. The attention was intoxicating, feeding something inside her she hadn't even known existed.

Encouraged by the growing enthusiasm, she pressed her body against the pole, the cool steel a stark contrast to her heated skin. She let herself move instinctively, sliding down, her thighs gripping the smooth metal as she rocked against it. Her full breasts, still barely concealed beneath her thin black dress, pressed around the pole as she dragged herself upward again, her hips rolling in slow, sensual waves.

A chant started low but grew louder with each passing second.

"More... more... more!"

The demand sent a thrill up Beth's spine. She had never felt so exposed, so *desired*, and yet, not a single part of her wanted to stop. The power coursing through her was electric, addictive. Every movement, every teasing grind against the pole was met with another round of applause, another hungry cheer urging her to go *further*.

She paused, her breath coming in quick, shallow gasps as she reached for the thin spaghetti straps of her dress. Her hands trembled—not with hesitation, but with exhilaration. Slowly, she slid the straps down her shoulders, feeling the fabric loosen, gravity pulling it lower. The silky material slipped over her full breasts, baring them completely to the crowd.

A wave of noise erupted from the audience.

Steve sat frozen, gripping the edge of the table so tightly his knuckles turned white. His wife—his once *modest*, *reserved* wife—was standing in the middle of the club, completely topless, owning the room like she had been *born* for this.

Beth's nipples were tight, aching points, her skin flushed from the heat of her performance. She could feel the air against her bare breasts, the way every eye in the room was locked onto her. The knowledge sent a deep pulse of arousal through her, making her stomach clench, her thighs press together.

She wasn't just *dancing* anymore.

She was *performing*.

She *wanted* them to look.

She wanted them to *see her*.

The crowd's cheers spurred her on, and without another thought, she let her dress slip past her hips. The moment it pooled at her feet, exposing the thin, soaked thong that barely covered her, the club erupted into *pure chaos*.

Beth closed her eyes, letting the sensation of absolute freedom wash over her. The lights, the music, the overwhelming sense of being desired—it all fused into one intoxicating, heady mix. She leaned back against the pole, letting the cool metal press against her heated skin as she moved, her body rolling, teasing, *inviting*.

She dragged the pole between her legs, letting it glide against the damp fabric of her thong, feeling every electrifying sensation. She arched, her breasts swaying with each movement, her nipples tightening further as she lost herself in the sheer *pleasure* of it all.

Steve still hadn't taken a breath.

His chest rose and fell in deep, measured breaths as he watched her, utterly captivated. He had *never* seen Beth like this—so uninhibited, so *raw*. It was as if she had shed every part of herself that had once been cautious, stepping into a version of herself that was *entirely new*.

The music swelled to a final, pulsing crescendo. Beth dropped to her knees, her thighs parted as she slid to the floor, her head falling back, her body glowing with sweat and arousal. The club *exploded* with applause, the standing ovation shaking the room.

Somewhere through the haze, Beth registered movement. The emcee stepped forward, extending a hand to help her up. She took it, her fingers still trembling slightly, her pulse roaring in her ears. He bent down, scooping up her dress before handing it to her.

Beth hesitated, the weight of what she had just done settling over her. But instead of fear, instead of regret, there was *something else*.

Pride.

Power.

Excitement.

She turned her gaze toward the table where Steve, Rich, and Chloe sat.

Chloe's smirk was *pure satisfaction*, her eyes gleaming with something close to admiration. Rich looked *wrecked*, his jaw tight, his body visibly reacting to everything he had just seen.

But Steve—*her husband*—was what sent another shiver through her.

He sat completely still, his fingers still gripping the table, his pupils blown wide. His chest rose and fell slowly, deeply, his entire body tense as he *devoured* her with his gaze. There was something in his eyes she had *never* seen before.

Possession.

Desperation.

Pure, unfiltered *lust*.

Beth's stomach clenched in anticipation.

Then, with a slow, knowing smile, she took her dress, turned, and let the emcee guide her behind the curtain.

Beth reappeared several minutes later, still wearing her dress but now with a radiant glow that hadn't been there before. Her smile was wide, her skin still flushed from the rush of the dance, the applause, and the heat of being so openly *desired*.

She slid into her seat, taking a slow sip of her now-diluted drink. The ice had melted, but she barely tasted it—her senses were still buzzing, her body still *thrumming* from everything that had just happened.

Rich was the first to break the silence, his voice tinged with something close to *awe*. "You were *fantastic*, Beth," he blurted, shaking his head. "That was even *hotter* than last night."

Chloe nodded eagerly, leaning in. "No need for a vote, honey. You *won*—hands down. The second you lost that dress, the contest was *over*." She smirked, swirling what remained of her drink. "You *had* me rooting for you, and then when you let it all *drop*—well, let's just say, I almost got up there *with* you."

Beth turned to Steve, her heart pounding as their eyes met.

There was something *intense* in his gaze—something that sent another wave of heat down her spine.

"I guess I went a bit *too* far," she started, her voice softer now, testing his reaction.

Steve didn't let her finish. His hand found her thigh beneath the table, warm and firm against her skin, sliding just *high enough* to make her breath catch. "You were *unbelievable*, babe," he murmured. "I'm so *proud* of the way you danced. I don't know how much *harder* I would've gotten if you'd removed your thong..."

Beth let out a slow, shaky breath, her thighs pressing together instinctively. *He wasn't mad.* In fact, he was *so far* from mad.

Relief flooded her, mixed with something deeper, something *needier*. "I was afraid you'd be upset," she admitted, her fingers playing with the edge of her dress. "But once I got started... I just *couldn't stop* myself." She swallowed, feeling the flush creep down her neck. "I'll admit... it was a complete *turn-on* to do what I did."

Chloe's eyes gleamed at the confession, her interest visibly piqued. She *understood* exactly what Beth meant. That *exhilaration*, that *thrill* of exposing yourself, of being *wanted* by so many people at once—it was something she had embraced long ago. Now, she could see it awakening in *Beth*, too.

"Shall we go back upstairs... perhaps to one of the *private rooms*?" Chloe suggested, her voice sultry, playful.

Beth hesitated, then shook her head. "I need more time," she admitted, her fingers tightening around Steve's hand. "And I think I'd like to go back to your place now. Steve and I have some... *unfinished business*." She bit her lip before adding, "Maybe we can come back tomorrow if the club is open."

Chloe tilted her head but didn't push. Instead, she smiled knowingly. "Sure. Most anything we can do *here*, we can do at home *too*." She let her gaze linger on Beth. "Maybe it's just too soon for you to try more than just *dancing* in front of strangers. You're not nervous when it's just *us*, are you?"

Beth exhaled slowly. "No, I guess not," she admitted. "We've already *seen* each other. And we're *friends*, so it *is* different." She hesitated. "I just don't want to spoil your fun here at the club. If you and Rich want to stay—"

"Don't be *silly*," Rich cut in. "We can come back *any time*. If you'd rather go home to play, we'll *pay the bill and head for the house, pronto*." He winked. "Maybe you'll be kind enough to give us an *encore*."

Beth laughed, shaking her head at his playful lechery. "I'm *so* horny right now... I might do *even more*," she teased, letting her eyes flick toward Steve.

The moment the taxi doors shut, the energy inside shifted—*tightened*. The small, dimly lit space seemed to amplify the *heat* crackling between them, the remnants of Beth's performance still thick in the air.

Beth's body was *humming*, her nerves still *raw* from the adrenaline coursing through her veins. The way Steve had looked at her—his eyes dark, *devouring*—had set something loose inside her, something *restless*. She didn't *think*, didn't *hesitate*. Instead, her fingers went straight for the zipper of his slacks, her movements bold in a way they never would have been before tonight.

Steve inhaled sharply, shifting in his seat as she pulled his cock free. He was already *achingly hard*, the thick weight of him twitching against her palm. She wrapped her fingers around him, stroking him *slowly* at first, just enough to make him *twitch*.

Chloe let out a soft, approving hum beside her. "Mmm..." she murmured, leaning in slightly, her breath warm against Beth's cheek. "Look at that. You've got him so worked up already."

Beth *shivered*.

Chloe was *so close*—closer than she'd ever been to another woman like this. And then, before she could fully process it, Chloe's hand moved, skimming over Beth's bare shoulder before sliding down to *cup* her exposed breast.

Beth *froze*.

The sensation sent a sharp *jolt* through her—both physical and mental. Her breath hitched, her pulse *skipping* as she struggled to *process* what was happening.

Chloe's touch was *light*, teasing, her fingers brushing lazily over Beth's nipple in a way that sent tiny *pulses* of heat straight through her core. It was shocking—*wrong*, almost—but at the same time, the slow, *sensual* drag of her nails across Beth's sensitive skin wasn't... *unpleasant*.

Beth's first instinct was to *pull away*, but her body betrayed her, her nipples tightening *further* beneath Chloe's touch.

Chloe chuckled softly, clearly aware of Beth's sudden tension. "Relax, sweetheart," she purred, giving her nipple a playful flick. "You're *so* sensitive... I love that."

Beth *sucked in a breath*, her fingers tightening around Steve's cock, her mind *reeling*. She wasn't into *women*—had never even *thought* about it before. And yet, the *sheer intimacy* of Chloe's touch, the *deliberateness* of it, sent another deep pulse of something *dangerous* through her.

But before she could dwell on it *too* much, Steve *groaned*, his hips twitching beneath her grip.

"Fuck, Beth..." he rasped, his fingers digging into the seat.

Chloe let her hand slide down Beth's ribs, then across her stomach, before finally pulling away. "God, he's so *thick*," she mused, her eyes locked onto Beth's hand as it worked over Steve's swollen shaft. "I bet that feels *amazing* when he's inside you."

Beth's *face burned*, but the compliment sent a fresh rush of *heat* straight between her thighs.

Steve let out another ragged breath, his head tipping back against the seat as Beth's strokes grew more *urgent*.

She could *feel* how close he was—the way his body tensed beneath her touch, the way his cock twitched against her palm. She *knew* his tells, *knew* the way his breathing *hitched* just before he came, but tonight, it was happening *so fast*.

Beth squeezed him just a little tighter, pumping him *harder*, her thumb dragging over his slick head.

"Shit—Beth—"

It *hit* him.

His body jerked, his thighs tensing beneath her as his climax *ripped* through him.

It happened *so quickly*, too *quickly*, and for a second, he looked almost *shocked* himself as the first hot pulse of his release spilled across her fingers.

Beth *gasped*, feeling the sudden warmth against her hand.

Chloe's *eyes widened*, then she burst into laughter, clapping her hands together as Steve let out a deep, *frustrated* groan.

"Oh my *God*," she *cackled*, shaking her head. "That was *adorable*."

Steve gritted his teeth, running a hand over his face as he *recovered*. "Jesus Christ…" he muttered, his voice laced with both *relief* and *embarrassment*.

Beth blinked, still gripping him, her fingers sticky with his release.

Chloe *grinned*, leaning in closer. "I guess Beth's little show *really* did a number on you, huh?"

Rich, sitting across from them, was *barely holding it together*. His hand was resting on his thigh, his fingers *visibly* flexing against the fabric of his pants. "Damn," he murmured, shaking his head. "I don't blame you, man. That was fucking *hot*."

Steve let out a slow exhale, finally opening his eyes to meet Beth's. There was something *almost apologetic* in his gaze, but also… *something else*.

Something *possessive*.

Something *hungry*.

Beth, her own body *aching* with unfulfilled need, felt another rush of *power* flood through her.

She had *never* made him come so *quickly* before. Had never seen him so *completely undone* by her.

And knowing that she *could*—that she *had*—sent another deep, *thrilling* pulse through her core.

Chloe reached forward, grabbing a napkin from the seat pocket before offering it to Steve with a playful smirk. "Here," she teased. "Clean yourself up, stud."

Steve grumbled something under his breath but took it, shaking his head as he *adjusted* himself.

Beth, still *flustered*, wiped her hand on the corner of her dress, her heart still *pounding*.

Chloe leaned in again, dropping her voice so only Beth could hear. "You know," she murmured, "if you ever want to *practice* teasing him like that… I'd be *happy* to give you some pointers."

Beth's stomach *clenched*.

She had *no idea* how to respond to that.

And somehow, she *knew*—this night was far from over.

THE ONE MORE

"It's still early," Rich announced as he moved toward the bar, reaching for a fresh bottle of whiskey. The clink of ice in the glasses punctuated his words as he began pouring. "I say we have some more fun." He smirked, glancing toward Beth and Steve. "I couldn't see much in the rearview mirror, but I know I missed out on something good," he added with a chuckle.

Beth, still feeling the residual *buzz* of the night, plopped down onto the couch with a soft groan. "Yeah, I *need* another drink after everything that happened tonight," she admitted, running a hand through her hair. Her skin still tingled from Steve's earlier touch, and her mind was *still reeling* from the fact that she had *completely let go* in front of a room full of strangers.

Chloe giggled, curling up beside her, her body still *vibrating* from the night's excitement. "Oh, at one point, *you* were the *hit* of the show, Beth," she teased. "That crowd *loved* you. And trust me... so did *we*."

Beth flushed at the memory, her thighs instinctively pressing together. The heat of those eyes on her, the pulse of the music, the *power* of being *wanted*—it had all been intoxicating.

"I *couldn't* believe she did it," Steve chimed in, his voice carrying a mix of pride and lingering *awe*. "And for a second, I really thought she might get *wild* upstairs."

Beth turned her head to look at him, arching an eyebrow. "I think you would have *liked* that," she teased, her voice light but edged with something *knowing*.

Steve didn't even *hesitate*. "Oh, *I know* I would have."

Rich, returning with the drinks, let out a *low chuckle*. "You're not the *only* one." He handed out the glasses, his fingers *brushing* Beth's for a fraction of a second longer than necessary as he passed hers to her.

Beth pretended not to notice the way his gaze lingered, instead taking a *generous* sip of her drink, the burn of whiskey doing little to cool the heat still *thrumming* in her veins.

Chloe tilted her head playfully. "Alright, *real talk*—what was your *favorite* part of tonight's… activities?" She directed the question at Steve first, her eyes gleaming with mischief.

Steve hesitated just long enough to make Beth's stomach *tighten*, but when he spoke, his voice was *firm*. "Beth's dance," he said, his gaze locked onto her. "It was such a *turn-on* for me to see her doing that in front of so many people." He paused, his lips curving into a smirk. "And to see how much she *liked* it."

Beth's breath *hitched*, her body warming under his stare.

Chloe let out an approving hum before shifting her focus. "*And you*, Chloe?"

"The same," she said without missing a beat. "Watching Beth get so *down and dirty* up there was the *hottest* thing I've seen in a while. I *wanted* to be up there *with* her," she admitted with a teasing grin, biting her lip. "*That*… and the upstairs show with the two women." She *blushed* slightly at her own admission, but her eyes *dared* anyone to challenge her.

"I *loved* it all," Rich declared, his voice rich with satisfaction. "The *dancing, the sucking, the fucking*—it was *all* great." He took a *long* sip of his drink, letting his words settle in the air.

Beth felt another *wave* of heat roll through her, the sheer *bluntness* of Rich's statement sending a small shiver down her spine. She wasn't sure if it was the alcohol, the night's events, or something *else*, but there was no denying the *thrill* that came with being so openly *desired*.

Chloe stretched lazily, rolling her shoulders. "Well," she purred, "the *show* must go on." She glanced around the room, her smile full of wicked promises. "So, *what* shall we do next, gang?"

Rich didn't *miss a beat*. He leaned forward, his grin bordering on *filthy*. "Let's all get naked," he suggested smoothly. "I think we all want to see some *tits and ass*."

Beth *gasped*, choking slightly on her drink, but before she could react, Chloe turned toward Rich, her lips curving into an amused smirk.

"You *first*," she challenged, arching an eyebrow. "Come on, big boy. *Show us what you've got*."

Rich grinned. "Oh, I *thought* you'd never ask."

Beth's pulse *skipped*, her fingers tightening around her glass as she realized—this night was *far* from over.

Rich didn't *hesitate*. With an easy confidence, he grabbed the hem of his shirt and pulled it over his head in one smooth motion, revealing the defined lines of his toned chest. His hands went straight to his belt, undoing it with a flick of his wrist before unzipping his slacks and letting them drop to the floor. Shoes and socks followed, leaving him in nothing but his underwear—*briefly*.

Beth barely had time to register what was happening before Rich hooked his thumbs into the waistband of his boxer briefs, his eyes *locked* onto hers as he slowly pushed them down his muscular legs. His cock—already semi-hard—sprang free, thick and growing by the second as he stepped out of his discarded clothing.

Beth swallowed hard, her fingers tightening around the glass in her lap.

Rich was *completely* naked.

And he *wasn't shy* about it.

His cock twitched slightly as it continued to stiffen under her gaze, and for a moment, Beth wondered if he had been *half-hard this whole time.*

"Okay, *Steve*, your turn," she urged playfully, trying to keep her voice *light*, as if the sight of her husband's best friend standing naked in front of her wasn't *doing* something to her.

Steve exhaled, running a hand through his hair before standing. Unlike Rich, his movements were slower, less theatrical. He peeled off his shirt and stepped out of his slacks, then hesitated for a fraction of a second before finally pushing his briefs down his hips.

Beth immediately *noticed* the difference.

Steve's cock—still *soft* from his climax in the taxi—rested between his thighs, noticeably thick but not yet showing any signs of rising to the occasion.

Rich, on the other hand, was already *fully erect.*

Beth's breath *hitched*, her thighs pressing together instinctively as she tried *not* to compare them—but it was impossible *not* to notice.

Steve sat back down beside her, his thigh brushing against hers. He *must* have realized the contrast too, because as soon as he settled next to her, he made a small, almost *defensive* gesture—his legs shifting slightly to make himself appear more relaxed, as if his lack of arousal didn't *bother* him.

Beth felt an odd *twist* in her stomach.

Not *pity*, exactly—Steve was never insecure about himself—but she knew that the *suddenness* of his earlier climax had caught him off guard, and now, surrounded by all this tension, his body wasn't *quite ready* to jump back into action.

"Okay," Steve said, his tone casual but *pointed*, as if daring *someone* to comment on the obvious. "We did as we were told. *What's* going to be our reward?"

Chloe's lips curled into a *slow, wicked* smile as she set her drink down and turned toward Beth.

"Let's give them a *lap dance*," she suggested, her voice dripping with mischief. She reached for Beth's hand, lacing their fingers together. "Maybe we'll give them *more* than one."

Beth's stomach *tightened*.

The way Chloe said it—so *confident*, so *teasing*—sent a sharp thrill through her, one she wasn't quite sure how to process.

Her eyes flicked toward Steve, then to Rich, whose erection *hadn't faded in the slightest*.

Both naked husbands were placed in deep, plush chairs, their positions almost deliberately staged—facing each other, mirroring the other's anticipation. Rich, still fully erect, lounged back confidently, his fingers draped over the armrests, while Steve, now semi-hard, kept his posture more composed, his thighs slightly spread, his cock beginning to show signs of life again but not yet matching Rich's full arousal.

Chloe moved to the sound system, selecting a slow, sensual track. The heavy beat pulsed through the dimly lit room, filling the space with an almost hypnotic rhythm. Beth felt a flutter of nerves in her stomach. She had agreed to this—had let herself be swept up in the intoxicating thrill of the night—but now, standing here, watching Chloe already swaying to the music, she felt a tangle of emotions she wasn't entirely sure she could control.

Steve hadn't been hard at first, and in some strange way, that had reassured her. It had reminded her that despite all the teasing and the eroticism of the night, he was still hers, still tethered to her in a way that felt familiar. But now, as she and Chloe moved toward their respective husbands, as she climbed onto Steve's lap, she knew her goal was to get him hard again. And that changed everything.

Beth started slow, letting her thighs spread over Steve's lap as she straddled him, feeling the warmth of his skin, the slight twitch beneath her as she ground down experimentally. His hands found her waist, gripping lightly as she rocked, the thin sheen of sweat on his chest telling her that, despite his earlier release, his body was waking up again. She bit her lip, moving more deliberately, rolling her hips in time with the music, rubbing the growing weight of him against her inner thigh. Steve groaned softly, his grip tightening, and Beth felt the first real throb against her.

Across the room, Chloe had wasted no time with Rich. She owned the space, her confidence electrifying as she moved against her husband's cock, her hands freely exploring, teasing him, her dress riding up higher and higher. Beth tried to focus on her own dance, on Steve, but she couldn't ignore the glances Rich kept stealing in her direction, the way his eyes lingered on her body as she moved.

The song swelled, the beat heavier, dirtier. Beth leaned into Steve's ear, brushing her lips against his skin as she whispered, "You like this, don't you?" His hands tightened on her waist. "You know I do," he murmured, his voice hoarse. Beth smirked, dragging her nails down his chest. She could feel him hardening now, his cock no longer just semi-hard, but thick and ready. Mission accomplished.

But then—Chloe stood.

Beth barely registered what was happening until Chloe turned toward her, a wicked gleam in her eye. She reached out, motioning for Beth to switch partners.

Beth froze.

For a split second, her mind blanked, her body reacting before her brain caught up. Her thighs tensed, her breath hitched, her hands tightened on Steve's shoulders. Switch. As in—swap. With Rich.

Her stomach tightened, her heartbeat hammering against her ribs. Chloe's suggestion felt like a wall she hadn't even realized she was approaching until it was right there in front of her. Dancing? Teasing? Even the lap dances had been within the bounds of excitement, of pushing limits without completely breaking them.

But this?

This was the edge of something else.

Beth turned her head toward Steve, searching his face for any sign of hesitation. But there was none. His gaze flickered toward Chloe—Chloe, who was already moving toward him, already sliding onto his lap before Beth could process it fully. And that was when the first sharp spike of fear hit her. Not because she didn't trust Steve. Not because she wasn't aroused.

But because she suddenly realized she had no idea what this meant.

She liked the teasing. She liked the way Steve had gotten so turned on watching her. But seeing Chloe grinding against him? That was different. And Rich—waiting for her—was different, too.

Beth's pulse roared in her ears. Her body was still thrumming from the high of the night, from the thrill of Steve's hands on her, from the power she had felt stripping down in front of strangers. But this? This felt like stepping into unknown territory.

Chloe's voice broke through the noise in her head. "Come on, Beth," she purred, her lips curling into a knowing smirk. "Don't be shy."

Beth swallowed, her throat suddenly dry.

Steve was already hard again. Rich was waiting.

The music pulsed.

And she had a decision to make.

As Beth settled onto Rich's naked lap, a slow, delicious heat coiled inside her. His hands instinctively found her soft breasts, cupping them possessively as he pulled her close, their bodies molding together. Through the fabric of her dress, she felt the rigid press of his arousal, undeniable proof of the effect she was having on him. A shiver of satisfaction ran through her, heightening the anticipation.

Rich's hands slid beneath her top, his touch both eager and deliberate. When his fingers found the sensitive peak of her nipple, rolling it between them, Beth exhaled a trembling sigh.

A low, throaty purr escaped her lips. "Oh, God," she breathed, surrendering to the sensation as she leaned further into her friend's husband, her body reacting to his every caress.

Across from them, Chloe was lost in the same erotic haze, her eyes dark with lust as she watched Rich pleasure Beth. The intimate scene sent jolts of heat straight between her legs. She shifted against Steve, her husband's stiff cock pressing insistently against her through the thin barrier of her dress. Desire surged through her—she needed more. Reaching for his hand, she guided it to her firm breast, a silent invitation for him to share in the arousal humming between them.

"Let's get jiggy," Chloe purred as the next song pulsed through the air, its hypnotic rhythm fueling the heat between them. She sprang from Steve's lap, her movements fluid and unashamed, stripping off her top in one swift motion. Her breasts, firm and tantalizing, caught the dim light as she faced Beth with a wicked grin. "Come on, Beth," she encouraged, her voice husky with desire.

With a teasing smirk, Beth followed suit, pulling off her top and revealing herself in the flickering light. Their bare skin gleamed with heat and anticipation as they returned to their respective partners, their bodies moving with the tempo, grinding seductively. The men's hands roamed freely—grasping, kneading, claiming—while mouths sought out hardened peaks, tasting, teasing. The air was thick with the scent of arousal, the erotic pulse of the music amplifying every electrified touch.

As Beth's fingers slid down, she found Rich's swollen length, her grip firm and teasing as she stroked him. Across from them, Chloe let out a soft moan, mirroring her friend's pleasure as her hands wrapped around Steve's throbbing shaft. The men groaned in unison, hips lifting toward the eager touch of their wives and their willing companion.

Then, as if caught in a shared fever, Chloe rose, her body gleaming with anticipation as she slipped off the rest of her clothes. Naked and unrepentant, she straddled her husband, taking him inside her in one fluid motion. A gasp of pleasure left her lips as she moved, matching the intoxicating beat of the music.

Beth watched her friend's brazen display, a fresh wave of desire making her core clench with need. Her hands trembled slightly as she shed the final layers of clothing. The cool air kissed her bare skin, but it was nothing compared to the heat between her legs. She turned to Steve, her eyes dark with hunger as she took his cock in her fingers, guiding him to her aching entrance.

A deep, familiar pleasure engulfed her as she sank down onto him, her body stretching to accommodate his thickness. A low, satisfied moan escaped her as she rocked against him, feeling the delicious friction. Steve's lips found her nipple, sucking it into his mouth as his hands dug into her hips, urging her to move faster, to take more.

By now, Beth's body was betraying her, her arousal pooling between her thighs, slick and undeniable. She had never felt this uninhibited before, never so utterly possessed by desire. The timid restraint that usually held her in check had vanished, replaced by something raw, something reckless. She locked eyes with Chloe, reading the same determined hunger reflected back at her.

For so long, they had danced around this moment, circling the forbidden, flirting with the idea but never quite crossing the line. But tonight, hesitation was a thing of the past. Tonight, they would finish what had been left unresolved far too many times before.

Beth turned to Steve, placing her hands on his broad shoulders, steadying herself. The anticipation in his eyes sent another rush of heat straight to her core. Leaning in, she kissed him deeply, their mouths clashing with feverish need. Then, with a slow, deliberate motion, she lifted herself off his lap, feeling the delicious drag of his cock as it slipped from her soaked folds. A shudder of pleasure rippled through her as she moved aside.

The moment Beth shifted, Chloe took her place, her bare thighs straddling Steve's lap, her body hovering just inches above his rigid shaft. She hesitated, savoring the moment, letting the electricity of anticipation coil between them.

"Hold him up for me, Beth," she murmured, her voice breathy, edged with desire.

Beth didn't hesitate. She sank onto one knee beside them, her fingers wrapping around her husband's slick, pulsing length. The contrast was intoxicating—her touch firm, his skin fever-hot, the tip of his cock glistening with her arousal. As she guided him forward, she watched, entranced, as Chloe's swollen lips parted, the head of Steve's cock nudging insistently against her glistening entrance.

Beth's breath caught. She had imagined this moment before, fantasized about it in the safety of her own mind—but nothing compared to witnessing it up close. The sight of her husband's thick shaft slowly breaching her best friend sent a wicked thrill through her, something primal and exhilarating.

For a moment, she was so lost in the vision, so mesmerized by the wet, intimate connection between them, that she didn't realize her fingers were still pressed between Steve and Chloe. She could feel everything—the heat, the slickness, the pulse of arousal binding them together. The sheer intimacy of it sent a jolt through her, snapping her back to reality.

With a shaky breath, she pulled her hand away and pushed herself upright, using Steve's shoulder for balance. As she did, her gaze flickered up to meet his.

His expression was unreadable, his eyes dark and wide with something between awe and disbelief. He was biting his lower lip, his body taut with restraint. Beth realized then—this was the first time he had felt Chloe, the first time he had been inside her.

And he was holding his breath.

Beth's pulse pounded in her ears. This was happening. There was no turning back now.

Turning her attention away, Beth locked eyes with Rich, who was leisurely stroking his long, thick shaft, his lips curled into a knowing smile. The dark hunger in his gaze sent a shiver of anticipation down her spine.

"Come to me, Beth," he coaxed, his voice thick with desire. "I've been waiting a long time."

Her gaze dipped to his hand, to the rigid length of him, and a rush of conflicting emotions swirled inside her. She had imagined this moment before—wondered how Rich might feel, how his size would compare to Steve's. Would his extra length hurt, or would she miss the intoxicating stretch of her husband's girth? Would he be able to give her something she never even knew she needed? A knot of fear, curiosity, and raw desire tightened in her core.

Beside her, Chloe let out a breathless moan as she continued to ride Steve, her nails digging into his shoulders. "Oh fuck, Steve," she panted, rolling her hips in slow, deliberate circles. "You feel so thick, stretching me so good... I can feel every inch of you filling me up." Her voice was needy, trembling with pleasure.

Steve groaned at her words, gripping Chloe's hips tighter, driving himself deeper into her. His eyes fluttered shut, lost in the sensation.

Beth stole a glance at her husband, watching as he surrendered to Chloe's touch. It was a strangely erotic sight—her best friend so completely enraptured by the very thing she had always known and loved about Steve.

Heart pounding, she turned back to Rich and, without a word, moved toward him.

"Climb aboard," Rich teased, tugging gently on her hands, guiding her onto his lap.

Beth straddled him, her body taut with anticipation. The moment his fingers slid between her folds, parting them, seeking her entrance, a desperate moan escaped her lips. He found the spot effortlessly, his thick, rounded head pressing against her slick opening.

She gasped as he pushed forward, stretching her with just an inch of his impressive length.

"Please be gentle, Rich," she whispered, her voice unsteady. "Go slow. I'm not used to one like yours."

Her plea sent a sharp pulse of arousal through Steve. His cock twitched inside Chloe at the thought of his wife struggling to take another man's size, of her realizing just how different it would feel.

Meanwhile, Chloe's movements quickened. She was riding Steve with slow, deliberate thrusts, her inner walls gripping him tightly, milking him with every motion. She arched her back, her breath coming in gasps. "Oh God, you're filling me so deep," she moaned.

Beth, lost in her own sensations, whimpered as Rich guided her down further, his hands cupping her breasts, kneading them as he controlled her descent. Another inch pushed into her, then another, his length sinking into her inch by inch.

Beth shuddered, gripping his shoulders. "Oh my God," she

gasped. "You're so... long. I've never felt anything this deep before."

Rich groaned, holding her still, savoring the tight squeeze of her around him. "You're taking me so well, Beth," he murmured, his thumbs brushing over her hardened nipples.

She let out a broken moan as another inch slid inside, making her core clench around him. She had never been filled like this before, never felt something pressing so deep inside her. The sensation was overwhelming—pleasure and pressure mingling, stretching her in ways she had never imagined.

"Oh, wait," Beth gasped, her fingers tightening on Rich's shoulders. "Not so fast, okay?"

He froze, his breath coming in slow, measured exhales as he let her adjust. Beneath his hands, her body trembled—not with fear, but with the intensity of it all. The stretch, the depth, the way he filled her in a way she had never known before.

She took a shaky breath, then another, and slowly, she allowed herself to relax. When the tension in her thighs eased, she sank just a little lower, taking him deeper, inch by inch.

"That's... that's all I'm used to," she confessed, her voice breathy, uncertain. She swallowed, then whispered, "Is there more?"

Rich's lips brushed against her ear, his voice thick with restraint. "Uh-huh," he murmured. "Quite a bit more. But take your time, babe."

His patience was agonizing, every nerve in his body screaming for release, but he knew she needed to ease into it. He wouldn't rush her—not when she was so warm, so impossibly tight around him. Instead, he let his hands wander, cupping the soft weight of her breasts, rolling her sensitive nipples between his fingers.

Beth's reaction was immediate. A sharp moan escaped her lips, her body arching into his touch. "Oh, yeah... touch me like that," she whimpered, and with a slow exhale, she allowed another inch to slide inside her.

Rich groaned softly, feeling the way her slick walls clung to him, gripping him as she took him deeper. He could barely think, barely hold back the need clawing at him, but he forced himself to stay still, letting her set the pace.

It took minutes—long, torturous, exquisitely slow minutes—but finally, he felt the soft press of her puffy mound against him. A shuddering breath left him. He was in. All the way.

Beth collapsed against his chest, her rapid breaths warming his skin, her soft breasts pressing against him as she trembled in his arms.

"Oh God," she murmured, her voice barely more than a whisper. "I feel so full." A shaky moan followed. "I didn't think I could take it all... but I guess I just did."

Rich exhaled sharply, his hands running soothingly over her back, holding her close as she adjusted to the overwhelming sensation. She was stretched around him, completely filled, and the sheer tightness of it made his pulse pound.

For a moment, they just stayed like that, bodies pressed together, breathing in unison. Then, slowly, Beth shifted, testing the way he felt inside her.

A tremor ran through her as she realized how slick she had become, how her body was molding around him, accommodating his size in a way she hadn't expected. Rich groaned as she moved just a little more, the delicious friction making his restraint unravel thread by thread.

His hands found the curve of her ass, gripping her gently as he lifted her, guiding her up just an inch before releasing her, letting her sink back down onto his thick, pulsing length.

Beth let out a broken moan as she settled onto him fully again, her fingers digging into his skin.

"Fuck," Rich growled under his breath. "That's it, babe. Just like that…"

The slow, teasing rhythm had begun, and neither of them would be able to hold back much longer.

"Mmm, yeah… feels so good," Chloe cooed, her voice thick with pleasure as Steve lifted her once more. The second descent made her gasp, his thick shaft stretching her, filling her so completely that she swore she could feel him in every inch of her body.

"Oh, fuck," she moaned as she settled onto him again, her inner walls fluttering from the deep intrusion. He felt impossibly thick inside her, his girth pressing into places she hadn't realized could feel so good.

Steve opened his eyes at the sound of her pleasure, the erotic sight before him making his pulse hammer. Just beyond Chloe, he could see Beth in Rich's arms, her body rising and falling, her slickness coating the thick length driving into her. The distinct, wet squelch of their joined bodies reached his ears, sending a sharp jolt of arousal through him.

The woman he loved—his beautiful Beth—was experiencing something entirely new, something he alone could never give her. And strangely, rather than jealousy, he felt a deep, overwhelming love swell in his chest.

Chloe's body reacted instantly to the shift in his cock. She felt him twitch, his arousal surging, and she grinned knowingly. She followed his gaze, watching as Steve took in the sight of his wife being taken by another man.

"This is so beautiful," Chloe whispered, her lips grazing his ear. "We're all so close right now... so connected." A little whimper followed as she rolled her hips, savoring the thick, pulsing fullness inside her.

Steve groaned, gripping her hips as she moved faster, grinding herself down onto him, taking him in completely.

"Oh God, Steve," she gasped, her breath hitching. "You're so thick... stretching me so much... I can feel every inch of you inside me." Her fingers dug into his shoulders as her body shuddered. "I love how you fill me up... so full... so deep..."

Her words sent a jolt of pleasure straight through him, and his restraint nearly shattered.

Chloe's movements grew frantic, urgent. Her moans turned into desperate cries as the pressure inside her coiled tighter and tighter.

And then—she shattered.

A tremor ran through her as her orgasm ripped through her body, waves of pleasure crashing over her in an unstoppable flood. Her slickness drenched him, her muscles clenching around his cock as she rode out the pleasure, gasping his name.

Steve groaned, his hands tightening on her hips, his entire body burning from the way she was pulsing around him. He had done this—he had made her lose herself completely.

The sight of Beth writhing on top of Rich, taking his long, deep strokes, had Steve teetering on the edge of insanity. His wife's moans were breathy, desperate, her body completely open for another man. He could see it—the way Rich's long shaft disappeared inside her, making her shudder as he bottomed out, stretching her in an entirely different way than Steve ever had.

The wet, obscene sounds of their bodies colliding filled the air, Beth's soaked pussy clinging to that deep-reaching cock as she rode him with increasing fervor.

Chloe was watching it, too, her own arousal dripping onto Steve's lap as she ground herself down onto his thick, pulsing length. She leaned in, her lips brushing his ear, her voice husky and taunting.

"Oh fuck, Steve," she purred, rolling her hips, letting him feel just how tight and wet she was around him. "You're so fucking thick—I can barely take you." She moaned, rocking against him, squeezing his cock with her slick walls. "God, I feel so full... you're stretching me open so good."

She circled her hips, taking him deeper, wringing every inch of pleasure from his swollen length. Then, she turned her head, her breath hitching as she watched Rich drive himself into Beth, his long cock vanishing into her soaked heat.

"Look at her," Chloe whispered filthily, her tongue flicking against Steve's earlobe. "Rich is fucking her so deep—she can feel him all the way inside. Bet she's never been filled like that before, huh? That long cock is hitting places even you can't reach."

Steve let out a strangled groan, his grip on her hips tightening as his cock twitched violently inside her.

Chloe smirked, feeling how close he was. "Mmm, but you love watching it, don't you?" she teased, her fingers grazing over his tight, aching balls. "Seeing Beth take that long cock all the way to the hilt while you're buried in me... fucking me so thick and deep... stretching me out like no one else ever could."

She clenched down around him, her pussy gripping him like a vice, milking his cock with every slick thrust.

That was it.

Steve groaned, his entire body locking up as he reached his breaking point. His cock throbbed wildly, and then—he exploded, spilling hot, thick ropes of cum deep inside Chloe's tight, trembling pussy.

Chloe gasped at the warmth flooding her, rolling her hips slowly to wring out every last drop. "Fuck, yes," she moaned, her nails digging into his shoulders. "Give me all of it, baby. Fill me up. Let me feel you dripping out of me."

Steve collapsed beneath her, breathless, overwhelmed, his mind fogged with the sheer intensity of his release.

Chloe rested her cheek against Steve's chest, their bodies still entwined, as they both watched the scene unfolding before them. Beth was still riding Rich, her body undulating in a desperate rhythm, taking his long, deep strokes with increasing abandon. Rich's hands were gripping her, spreading her open, and Steve could see how stretched she was, how completely she had surrendered to him.

Beth's mouth fell open, a strangled moan escaping as Rich's cock bumped the entrance of her cervix, pressing into the very depths of her womb.

"Oh, oh yeah... right there," she gasped, her body trembling. "Go easy, go easy, Rich," she begged, rising and falling on his long shaft, the deep penetration making her toes curl.

Rich groaned beneath her, his fingers digging into her ass. "You're the one moving," he panted. "Come on, Beth—fuck me with that hot, dripping pussy."

His filthy words sent a shockwave through her, igniting something primal. The hesitation in her movements disappeared, replaced with raw, unfiltered need. Beth's body took over, her hips rolling faster, harder, grinding down onto him with reckless abandon.

Her moans became louder, more desperate, her ass bouncing with every thrust. "Yes, oh yes, oh—oh, fuck," she whimpered against his shoulder, her fingers clutching at his back as her pleasure built to an unbearable peak. "Cum with me, cum with me," she gasped, her body convulsing, her orgasm crashing over her like a tidal wave.

Steve and Chloe watched as Rich threw his head back, his entire body going rigid.

"There he goes," Chloe murmured into Steve's chest, her voice dripping with sinful pleasure. "My husband is filling your wife with a huge load right at this moment."

Steve could only stare, breathless, as the moment stretched in slow motion. His sweet, loving wife—the woman he had made love to for years—was now trembling in another man's arms, accepting his cum deeper than Steve had ever reached himself.

Beth gasped as she felt it—the first hot spurt shooting deep inside her, then another, and another, coating her womb with thick ropes of another man's seed. Her body shuddered, clenching around him, milking every last drop as the warmth spread through her.

Rich groaned beneath her, his cock pulsing over and over as he emptied himself inside her, his grip tightening as he held her down, making sure she took it all.

Chloe grinned wickedly, shifting slightly against Steve's still-sensitive cock. "Mmm, look at her, baby," she whispered. "Your wife is so full of my husband's cum right now... it's leaking out of her, dripping all over his balls... making a fucking mess."

Steve swallowed hard, his arousal somehow spiking again despite having just climaxed, watching as Beth slowly lifted herself off Rich's still-hard length. Their combined fluids spilled from her, a glistening trail of evidence of what had just happened.

Rich exhaled sharply, his muscles finally relaxing, feeling the warm slickness pooling beneath them, soaking the seat of the chair in the aftermath of their raw, unrestrained passion.

Time seemed to stand still, the four of them tangled in a haze of exhaustion, satisfaction, and the undeniable thrill of what they had just shared.

Steve was overwhelmed with love for his wife. Though an initial flicker of jealousy had surfaced, it had quickly faded, replaced by something far deeper. Watching Beth surrender to another man, seeing the raw pleasure on her face, had been a revelation. He wasn't losing her—if anything, he had just witnessed her receive an incredible gift, an experience that had pushed her to new heights. And he had been privileged to watch every moment of it.

His thoughts drifted, and he became acutely aware of the lingering heat around his softening cock. Chloe was still wrapped around him, her tight, soaked pussy clinging to him in the aftermath of their own shared pleasure. A fresh wave of arousal stirred in his belly.

Chloe, too, was lost in thought. For so long, she had teased and flirted, stolen lingering glances, imagined what it might feel like to experience Steve fully. And now that it had happened, now that his thick length had stretched and filled her, she knew it had been worth every second of waiting.

She had often envied Beth—her luscious curves, her generous tits, the way men seemed to hunger for her. Chloe, with her smaller, more petite frame, had wondered how Steve might react to her, how she would feel beneath him, against him, taking him. It had almost become an obsession.

And now, she knew.

The room was thick with the scent of sex, the air still charged with the echoes of their pleasure. Their bodies hummed with the aftershocks, damp with sweat, hearts still thundering in the quiet.

Finally, after several minutes of slow, heavy breathing, Beth stirred. With languid movements, she rose from Rich's lap, his long shaft slipping free, leaving her empty, trembling, and utterly satisfied. A final trickle of warmth spilled from her as she moved, proof of what had just transpired.

She lowered herself onto the soft carpet, rolling onto her back with a satisfied sigh. Legs sprawled wide, her body glistened with sweat and arousal, utterly spent, unashamed, and beautifully wrecked. A lazy smile tugged at her lips as she exhaled slowly, her fingers brushing idly over her belly.

She had never felt so thoroughly used. So completely claimed.

Chloe watched Beth's slow, languid descent onto the carpet, her bare, glistening body sprawled in the aftermath of pleasure. A flicker of hunger flashed in Chloe's eyes as she licked her lips.

Without hesitation, she slid onto the floor, crawling forward on all fours, her movements slow, deliberate. Steve watched, his pulse quickening, as she closed the space between them.

The two women locked eyes, a silent exchange passing between them—understanding, curiosity, desire.

Chloe leaned in first, her breath warm against Beth's lips, and then they kissed. It was soft at first, exploratory, then deepened, tongues teasing, mouths parting in slow, unhurried seduction.

"That was so beautiful," Chloe murmured just loud enough for the men to hear, her voice thick with emotion and lingering lust.

Beth's lips curled into a weak but satisfied smile. "Thank you... for knowing. For being willing." Her words were cryptic, but Chloe understood.

Beth sighed, her fingers threading into Chloe's hair as she pulled her in for another lingering kiss. "I feel so good right now," she murmured against her lips, her body still humming from the waves of pleasure coursing through her.

Chloe's lips curled into a wicked smile. "I want you to feel even better," she whispered, trailing kisses along Beth's jaw before moving lower, her mouth seeking the delicate curve of her throat, her tongue flicking over the salty sheen of sweat on her skin.

Beth let out a soft, contented sigh as Chloe moved further, her lips finally capturing an already erect nipple. She suckled gently at first, her tongue swirling around the sensitive peak before pulling it between her lips, teasing it with slow, rhythmic flicks.

Rich and Steve sat in silence, mesmerized by the sight before them. Their wives—so familiar, yet so foreign in this intimate exchange—were wrapped in each other's touch, whispering, exploring. Their soft, sensual movements sent a fresh pulse of heat through both men, the remnants of their pleasure stirring back to life.

Chloe flicked her gaze up to Beth's, her lips still wrapped around her nipple. She released it with a soft pop, then leaned in close to her friend's ear, her breath warm and enticing.

"I want to taste," she whispered, the words dripping with sinful promise. "I want to taste you... and my Rich."

Beth's body tensed slightly at the confession, her breath catching as she turned her head, glancing first at her husband, then at Rich. Their eyes met, and a slow, knowing smile spread across her lips.

"Uh-huh," she moaned softly, the sound barely more than a whisper.

Chloe wasn't sure if that was an explicit invitation, but at this point, she wasn't waiting for further clarification. The ache inside her was too strong, the curiosity too overwhelming.

Positioning herself between Beth's parted thighs, Chloe lowered her body, inch by inch, until she was fully nestled between her friend's legs.

Her gaze dropped to the sticky mess left behind by her husband, glistening proof of the pleasure Beth had just experienced. Chloe's mouth watered at the sight, her breath shuddering as she leaned in closer.

Then, without hesitation, she pressed her lips to Beth's slick, swollen folds, tasting the mix of arousal and release, moaning softly as she finally indulged in the forbidden.

Beth's reaction was almost immediate. A gasp escaped her lips as her fingers tangled into Chloe's blonde hair, gripping tightly, guiding her deeper, her body arching in raw, unfiltered need. Her thighs spread wider, her hips lifting, pressing herself insistently against Chloe's eager mouth.

Chloe moaned at the intensity of Beth's response, loving the way her friend surrendered so easily to pleasure. She dragged her tongue slowly over Beth's swollen folds, savoring the intoxicating mixture of heat and slickness, the unmistakable taste of sex still lingering between her thighs.

Her nose brushed against Beth's clit, and the soft, throbbing nub twitched under the friction. Encouraged by the reaction, Chloe flicked her tongue along Beth's slit, teasing the tender flesh before diving deeper, parting the sticky folds with her lips.

The distinct flavor of Beth—mixed with the remnants of Rich's release—coated her tongue. The musky, heady scent filled her senses, making her clench with need as she lapped up every trace of their shared pleasure.

Beth whimpered, her breath hitching. "Oh, God, Chloe…" she moaned, her grip tightening in her friend's hair. Her body was still sensitive, every nerve alight from the orgasm Rich had just given her, but Chloe's mouth was relentless, determined to wring every last drop of pleasure from her.

Above them, Rich lay spent in his chair, his chest rising and falling with deep, steady breaths. He was completely drained, his body too satisfied to move, but his eyes were locked onto the scene before him. The sight of his wife between Beth's legs, her tongue working eagerly, her ass raised high in the air—it was undeniably erotic.

For Steve, however, the effect was even stronger.

The lingering thrill of the night, combined with the view of Chloe's glistening, upturned ass, sent a fresh jolt of arousal through him. He had just experienced one of the most intense orgasms of his life, but his body wasn't done yet—not with the way Chloe looked, positioned so perfectly before him, her petite frame spread out in wanton submission.

His hand drifted down, fingers wrapping around his length, stroking himself back to life. His breath grew heavier, the heat in his core reigniting as he watched Chloe devour his wife with slow, indulgent movements.

Beth moaned louder, her thighs trembling as Chloe's tongue flicked over her clit in rhythmic strokes. She gasped, her head tossing back against the carpet. "Oh, fuck, that feels so good… don't stop."

Chloe had no intention of stopping. She curled her tongue, dipping deeper into Beth's entrance, drinking in the wetness that continued to ooze from her. Her own body burned with need, her slick folds aching, clenching around nothing.

Steve's stroking quickened. His erection throbbed in his hand as he watched, anticipation building. He licked his lips, eyes locked onto Chloe's swaying hips, the perfect curve of her ass as it lifted invitingly before him.

And as he moved closer, he knew exactly what he wanted to do next.

Steve shifted forward, positioning himself between Chloe's spread legs, his newly hardened cock brushing against her slick folds. Without hesitation, he pushed inside her once more, groaning at the familiar, welcoming heat. Chloe moaned into Beth's trembling core, her body adjusting effortlessly to him, taking his full, thick length with a slow, deep thrust.

His hands moved to her ass, spreading her soft cheeks apart, exposing the tight ring of muscle between them. The sight of her, so completely open before him, sent another pulse of arousal through him.

With a deliberate slowness, he pressed his thumb against her back entrance, teasing the tight rim before pushing it inside.

Chloe grunted, then let out a low, shuddering moan as her body instinctively pushed back against him.

From his chair, Rich chuckled, his gaze fixed on the scene before him. "She likes it, but she says I'm too long for that," he mused, amusement and arousal lacing his voice.

Steve smirked, taking Rich's comment as permission to continue. He began moving his thumb in slow, controlled circles, working her open with careful patience. Chloe's breath hitched, but she didn't resist. If anything, she encouraged it, subtly rocking her hips back toward him.

Feeling her willingness, he withdrew his thumb and replaced it with two fingers, easing them inside her, stretching her further. Chloe whimpered into Beth's wetness, pushing back greedily.

That was all the invitation Steve needed.

Slipping his cock from her drenched pussy, he guided the swollen head to her now-loosened back entrance. He rubbed against her puckered hole, teasing her, feeling the resistance before pressing forward.

"Mmm... oh," Chloe mumbled, her voice muffled as she buried her face deeper into Beth's thighs.

Steve applied steady pressure, his thick cock forcing her open inch by inch. The tight heat gripped him fiercely as he breached her, the sensation almost overwhelming. Once past her sphincter, her body relaxed around him, allowing him to push in deeper, finally burying himself to the hilt.

A shuddering sigh left his lips. She was impossibly tight, the snug grip around his cock sending a delicious pulse of pleasure through his spine.

Rich exhaled, watching intently, his spent but still-stirring cock twitching at the sight.

"Not the first time this blonde has been ass-fucked," Steve murmured with a satisfied smirk as he began to move, slowly at first, then gradually increasing his pace, his thick shaft sliding in and out of her tight, glistening hole.

Chloe moaned, the pleasure-pain mix sending shivers through her. She clung to Beth's thighs, her mouth working her friend's sensitive folds even as Steve claimed her from behind. The combined sensations—being taken so completely, pleasing

Beth with her tongue—had her trembling, spiraling toward something deeper, more intense.

Steve's deep, steady thrusts only served to press Chloe's face harder into Beth's soaked mound, forcing her to take every drop of her friend's arousal. The desperate moans vibrating against Beth's sensitive flesh sent another jolt of pleasure through her, tipping her over the edge once more.

"Oh yes, yes, yes!" Beth squealed, her thighs trembling as a fresh wave of ecstasy crashed over her. Her fingers tangled in Chloe's blonde hair, holding her in place as her hips bucked, riding the blissful aftershocks.

The sight, the sounds, the raw, unrestrained pleasure of it all sent Steve spiraling toward his own release. The tight grip of Chloe's ass squeezed him mercilessly, and with a final deep thrust, his cock twitched violently. His breath caught in his throat as he spilled a diminished but still potent load inside her, each pulse sending another shudder through his already-overstimulated body.

Chloe whimpered beneath him, her mouth still working Beth's dripping folds even as she felt the last of Steve's warmth coat her insides, mixing with the slickness already leaking from her. She was completely spent, her body used, stretched, and thoroughly satisfied.

A few minutes passed in a haze of heavy breathing and lingering aftershocks before Rich's deep, commanding voice cut through the silence.

"Now that you've finished with Beth, come over here and clean me up."

Chloe blinked up at her husband, her lips glistening, her expression hazy with pleasure and exhaustion. Slowly, she peeled herself away from Beth's soft thighs and crawled toward

Rich, her body still trembling slightly.

Dutifully, she settled between his legs, lowering her mouth to his now-limp but still slick shaft. Her tongue flicked over him, lapping up the sticky remnants of their shared pleasure, savoring the combined taste of Beth and himself.

Rich sighed, running a lazy hand through her hair as she cleaned him thoroughly, her lips and tongue working with practiced precision.

Meanwhile, Steve sat back, running a hand through his damp hair. The break in the action gave him a chance to catch his breath—and to acknowledge the sticky reality of what had just transpired. His cock, still sensitive, twitched slightly as he looked down at himself, his skin glistening with the evidence of Chloe's surrender.

With a satisfied grunt, he pushed himself to his feet. "I'm gonna get cleaned up," he muttered, heading toward the bathroom to wash away the remains of the deep, filthy fuck he had just given Chloe.

As he stepped into the shower, letting the warm water cascade over him, he couldn't help but smirk.

Tonight had been beyond anything he had ever imagined.

"What now?" Rich asked, his fingers absently tracing lazy circles over Chloe's bare back as she lay curled up in his lap. The air was still thick with the scent of sex, bodies warm, limbs heavy with exhaustion. No one had bothered to dress after their incredible tryst.

Steve let out a deep breath, glancing at his friend before looking down at Beth, who lay nestled beside him on the couch. Her body was still flush with the afterglow, a faraway look lingering in her eyes.

"I don't know about the rest of you," Steve said, stretching his sore limbs, "but I'm exhausted. That was more exercise than I get in a month. I'm ready for bed."

Chloe lifted her head slightly, her expression thoughtful. "Maybe we should stay up and talk about things," she suggested tentatively, her voice softer now, as if reality was beginning to settle in.

Steve shook his head. "Let's talk tomorrow. This is too fresh right now." His voice was firm, decisive. "Let's go to bed."

Chloe smirked, a playful glint in her eyes. "Go to bed with whom?" she teased.

Before Steve could answer, Beth's voice cut through the room, soft but sure. "I'm tired now, but I'll be okay by morning."

Steve turned to look at her, a flicker of surprise passing through him. She met his gaze, and for a moment, he saw something there—a longing, a quiet plea, something deep and unspoken.

Beth hesitated, then licked her lips, inhaling as if bracing herself. "Maybe just for tonight?" she murmured.

Steve blinked. "Sleep with Rich?" His voice was quiet, careful, as if he wasn't sure he had heard her correctly.

Beth swallowed, her fingers toying with the edge of the blanket draped over her waist. "Only if it's okay with you, honey," she said, her voice barely above a whisper. She knew how out-of-character the request sounded, yet she also knew that she wanted to experience Rich's long cock at least once more. If not tonight, when?

Steve exhaled slowly, his mind racing. A part of him wanted to protest, but another part—the part that had watched her lose herself in pleasure, had seen the way her body responded to Rich

—understood.

He swallowed hard, then gave a slow nod. "Okay... just for tonight. I guess that would be okay, given what's already happened."

Chloe grinned, sliding off Rich's lap and stretching lazily. "I'll make sure you're not bored," she teased, winking at Steve.

Rich, sensing the tension, cleared his throat. "Steve's right. If nobody wants another drink, let's hit the hay... as they say."

Beth turned to her husband and cupped his face, kissing him long and deep. When she pulled back, her lips hovered near his, her breath warm against his skin. "It'll be okay, honey. You'll see," she whispered. "I love you for being so understanding."

Steve nodded, not trusting himself to speak.

Beth turned to Rich, then to Chloe, offering a small, knowing smile. "Just let me grab my toothbrush and lipstick, Rich. I'll be along shortly."

She stood, stretching with an easy grace, and began strolling toward the hallway that led to the master suite. Steve's eyes followed her, watching the gentle sway of her hips, the confidence in her step. The toothbrush in her hand seemed almost comically ordinary considering the intense, boundary-shattering night they had just shared.

A shiver ran through him, unexpected and undeniable.

Then, a small, soft hand touched his shoulder.

"Take me to bed, Steve," Chloe purred, her lips brushing the shell of his ear before pressing a kiss just below it.

His pulse quickened as he turned to her, seeing the promise in her gaze.

THE MORNING AFTER

Dawn eventually broke around nine o'clock the next morning, sunlight filtering through the curtains in soft, golden streaks. Steve stirred, stretching slightly before his hand brushed against warm, bare skin. For the first time in a long time, it wasn't Beth lying beside him.

His fingers trailed over a slender leg, smooth and toned. That's when the events of the previous night came rushing back into his conscious mind—the indulgence, the tangled bodies, the whispered moans, the breaking of unspoken boundaries.

Chloe.

She was awake but remained silent, letting him explore her with slow, curious touches. His hand traced over the gentle curve of her hip, the dip of her waist, the swell of her breast. Her skin was warm beneath his fingertips, still carrying the heat of the night before.

Finally, she spoke, her voice husky from sleep. "Good morning, sleepyhead. How do you feel this morning?"

Steve rolled onto his side, facing her. His eyes took in her tousled blonde hair, the faint smudges of lipstick still clinging to her lips, the dark streaks of mascara beneath her eyes. She looked spent, well-loved, and completely unashamed.

Chloe smiled, her fingers reaching out to brush lightly against his cheek.

"Okay, I guess," Steve murmured, still trying to untangle his thoughts, to reorient himself in this new reality.

"You'll feel better after coffee and some breakfast," she assured him, stretching her arms above her head, the movement making her bare skin shift enticingly against the sheets. "I don't know about you, but I'm starved and thirsty."

She leaned in, pressing a soft, lingering kiss to his lips before slipping from the bed, completely unbothered by her nudity.

Rising up on one elbow, Steve watched her saunter toward the bedroom door, the graceful sway of her hips hypnotizing.

Just before she disappeared down the hall, she glanced over her shoulder with a playful smirk. "Why don't you go wake up our spouses and tell them I'm making coffee?"

Steve remembered their earlier conversation. He recalled agreeing to change partners and being led by Chloe to the guest bedroom. The last thing he remembered was sinking into the mattress, exhaustion claiming him almost immediately.

"I must have gone right to sleep," he thought groggily, rubbing a hand over his face. "I hope Chloe wasn't disappointed with me." Tossing the sheet aside, he stood and shuffled to the bathroom, barely awake as he relieved himself. His stream seemed endless as he stood over the toilet, emptying his bladder while mulling over Chloe's suggestion from earlier.

"Guess I should wake them up, like she said," he muttered to himself, making his way toward the master suite. The door was open. That was the first thing he noticed. The second was what was happening inside.

Steve stopped dead in the doorway, his breath catching in his throat. Beth was on her knees in the center of the bed, her head bobbing between Rich's legs. His lovely wife was sucking Rich's cock.

His stomach twisted, a strange, heated feeling creeping through him as he stared at the scene before him. Rich lay sprawled against the pillows, his fingers tangled in Beth's hair, guiding her as she worked him with slow, eager movements. The slick, wet sound of her lips gliding along his length filled the room, mingling with the occasional soft moan Beth made as she took him deeper and deeper.

Steve's pulse pounded as he watched her mouth stretch around Rich's cock, her fingers wrapped firmly around the base, stroking in perfect rhythm. She looked hungry for it, completely lost in the act. A low groan rumbled from Rich's chest. "Oh, fuck… Beth, you feel amazing."

Steve swallowed hard, something hot curling in his gut. He had seen Beth give head before, but this was different. This wasn't obligation. This wasn't a quick warm-up before sex. She was devouring him.

Rich's hips twitched, his abs tensing, and Beth adjusted effortlessly, taking him even deeper. Steve watched, mesmerized, as her cheeks hollowed with each stroke, her tongue swirling around him with deliberate, practiced enthusiasm. His hands clenched at his sides. Had she ever done that for him?

Beth moaned softly around Rich's length, the sound sending another sharp wave of heat straight through Steve's body. His cock twitched despite the jealousy creeping into his chest.

"Oh, Beth… I'm close," Rich groaned, his voice strained. "Gonna cum."

Steve expected her to pull away, to finish him with her hand like she always had before. But she didn't. Instead, she moaned and sucked him harder, her fingers tightening at his base as if urging him to let go.

Steve's eyes widened, his breath stalling in his chest. Rich groaned deep in his throat, his fingers tightening in Beth's hair as his hips jerked. With a strangled gasp, he spilled into her mouth.

Steve's stomach dropped. Beth didn't pull away. She whimpered and swallowed. Every drop.

He stared in disbelief as Beth continued sucking, milking every last spurt from Rich's cock, her throat working in steady gulps. When she finally pulled back, she licked her lips before pressing a soft kiss to the tip.

His heart pounded in his ears. Beth had swallowed. For Rich. And not once, in all their years together, had she ever done that for him.

Something dark and complicated twisted inside him. He had agreed to share her. He had agreed to this.

So why the hell did it feel like he was the only one who had truly lost something?

The pair lay still, panting, as the aftershocks of their pleasure subsided. Beth wiped the corner of her mouth with the back of her hand, licking her lips as she settled onto the bed beside Rich. His chest rose and fell in steady waves, his body lax, completely spent from what she had just done for him. The room was thick with the scent of sweat and sex, the sheets tangled beneath them in the aftermath. Rich let out a long, satisfied breath before rolling onto his side, stretching lazily.

As Steve moved into the master bedroom, his body was tense,

his thoughts racing. His mind wanted to reject what he had just seen, but his cock told a different story. It was hard—achingly hard—and leading him toward the side of the bed, the raw imagery still playing in his head.

The pair on the bed seemed momentarily startled when he spoke. "Chloe's fixing coffee and some breakfast if you're interested." His voice came out steadier than he expected, masking the strange mix of jealousy, lust, and discomfort brewing inside him.

Rich smirked, stretching his arms above his head before throwing a lazy glance toward Beth. Beth, however, wasn't looking at Rich anymore. Her gaze had dropped lower—straight to Steve's throbbing erection.

Her lips curled slightly, her expression unreadable as she slowly let her eyes drift back up to his face. She smiled, soft and inviting, almost teasing. "Got a good morning kiss for me, honey?"

Steve hesitated, something about her tone sending a flicker of uncertainty through him. But habit—and love—overrode his instincts. Without thinking, he leaned down over her naked body and pressed his lips to hers in a slow, intimate kiss.

Beth moaned softly into his mouth, her lips parting slightly as she deepened it, her tongue teasing against his. He tasted something warm, something slightly different than usual. His brows furrowed slightly, but she kissed him harder, wrapping a hand around the back of his neck, holding him there.

Then, suddenly, it hit him.

The taste. The texture. The lingering warmth.

His stomach lurched as realization slammed into him like a freight train. It was Rich.

She had just swallowed his load. And now, she was feeding it to him.

Steve pulled back abruptly, his tongue instinctively running over his lips as his brain scrambled to process what had just happened. His eyes widened in disbelief, flicking between Beth's satisfied smirk and Rich's amused expression.

"The fuck, Beth?" he muttered, wiping his mouth with the back of his hand.

Beth only chuckled, reaching up to trace her fingers over his chest before sliding her hand down, wrapping her fingers around his rock-hard cock. She gave it a slow, deliberate stroke, her grip firm, teasing.

"Don't pretend you didn't enjoy watching," she murmured, her voice dripping with satisfaction.

Steve's jaw tensed, his body betraying him as his cock throbbed in her grasp. He wanted to deny it, wanted to push her hand away, but he couldn't.

Because deep down, she was right.

She always was.

As Steve helped his recently satisfied wife from the bed, Rich rolled off the other side, stretching before heading toward the kitchen to find Chloe. His long, soft cock flopped between his legs as he walked away, completely at ease with himself, leaving Steve standing there, stark naked, his own erection still aching.

Beth stretched languidly, letting out a contented sigh before looking at her husband with a teasing smirk. Without a word, she climbed back onto the bed, laying on her back, parting her legs slowly, deliberately.

Steve swallowed hard.

"Come here," Beth murmured, her fingers lazily tracing her own damp inner thigh.

Steve's body tensed. The remnants of the night were still on her—the musky scent of sweat and sex, the faint taste of another man still lingering on her lips. His thoughts swirled as he hesitated, but Beth's gaze held steady. There was no question in her eyes, no request. This wasn't a suggestion.

Slowly, he lowered himself to the edge of the bed, positioning himself between her spread thighs.

"Good boy," she murmured softly, running a hand through his hair before guiding him downward.

Steve inhaled sharply as his lips brushed against her warm, slick folds. The scent of their mixed arousal filled his senses, and for a brief moment, his mind rebelled. He couldn't believe this was happening—couldn't believe what he had watched her do just minutes ago.

His tongue flicked out hesitantly, tracing along her sensitive flesh. Beth moaned softly, stretching like a satisfied cat, completely comfortable in her own skin, completely unbothered by the situation.

As he licked, the words just slipped out.

"I... I can't believe you swallowed."

Beth exhaled a small, breathy laugh. "Mmm. I know."

Steve paused, his tongue hovering just above her clit. "You always said you hated it."

Beth let out a slow, indulgent sigh, shifting her hips slightly, urging him to keep going. Steve swallowed hard before resuming, his tongue pressing firmly against her swollen bud, waiting for her to explain.

"I do hate it," she admitted casually, as if they were discussing breakfast.

Steve's brow furrowed, his tongue slowing just enough to let his confusion be known. "Then... why?"

Beth propped herself up on her elbows, watching him with an amused glint in her eyes. "Because I wanted to."

He blinked up at her, licking hesitantly, his mind racing. "But if you hated the taste..."

Beth smirked, threading her fingers through his hair again, her nails scratching lightly against his scalp. "It wasn't about that," she murmured. "It was about power. In that moment, I had complete control over him. He was mine."

Steve's stomach clenched.

She pulled lightly on his hair, tilting his head up so their eyes met. "You really don't get it, do you?" she mused.

Steve did get it. He just didn't want to admit that he did.

Beth let her head fall back against the pillows, a low moan spilling from her lips as Steve continued lapping at her folds, working her with slow, deliberate strokes. Her hips lifted slightly against his mouth, guiding him, setting the pace.

Steve should have been disgusted. But his cock throbbed relentlessly, trapped between his own stomach and the bed. His jaw ached, his tongue burned, but he kept going, knowing this was what she wanted from him now.

When Beth came, she gasped, her back arching slightly, fingers tightening in his hair. Her thighs trembled as she shuddered through the waves of pleasure, her breath ragged as she slowly relaxed beneath him.

Steve waited.

She didn't move.

He lifted his head slightly, half-expecting her to return the favor. Half-expecting her to slide down the bed, take his still-hard cock into her warm, waiting mouth, finish him off.

Beth simply stretched, completely content, before swinging her legs over the side of the bed.

"I need a shower," she murmured, as if nothing had happened.

Steve stared. "Wait. That's it?"

Beth turned her head, raising an eyebrow at him. "What did you think was going to happen?"

His stomach clenched again.

She smirked, stepping toward the bathroom. "Come on," she called over her shoulder, not bothering to look back.

Steve hesitated, then followed.

By the time they were dry, the aroma of fresh-brewed coffee filled the air, luring them back to reality. Hand in hand, they walked down the hallway toward the kitchen.

Rich was already seated at the table, cup in hand, looking perfectly at ease. He smiled as his cute blonde wife stood at the stove, humming softly while flipping eggs, wearing nothing but an apron. The fabric barely covered her curves, the ties resting loosely at her back, her bare skin peeking out teasingly.

"Everything okay?" Rich asked casually, setting his mug down, his tone easy but his eyes searching.

Steve paused, his fingers briefly tightening around Beth's. He let the question hang for a moment, considering the answer.

"Yeah," he finally said, exhaling slowly. "We're fine. Just fine."

Beth squeezed his hand in silent reassurance.

Fine.

For now.

Rich grinned with relief, leaning back in his chair. "We are two very lucky fellows, you know," he said, lifting his coffee cup. "I hope we stay close friends forever."

"Me too, me too," Chloe agreed brightly, flipping the eggs in the pan with an easy, satisfied rhythm. The atmosphere in the kitchen was warm, relaxed, as if the night before had settled into something comfortable, something understood.

Steve gave a small nod, but his thoughts were elsewhere. His mind kept drifting back—to the taste Beth had left on his lips, to the way she had moaned when he had licked her clean, to the undeniable shift in their relationship. It wasn't jealousy anymore. It was something deeper, something he couldn't quite name.

Beth remained quiet as the others talked, stirring her coffee absently, her gaze distant. She was thinking. Weighing something. Finally, she cleared her throat, her voice soft but firm.

"I need to say something. I need to bring something out into the open. And, Rich, don't take this the wrong way, okay?"

Rich raised an eyebrow, setting his cup down. "Okay..." he said slowly, curiosity flickering in his eyes.

Steve tensed, watching his wife carefully. Something about her tone sent a strange, nervous flutter through his chest.

What was she about to say?

And why did he have the feeling that, whatever it was, it was about to change everything?

Beth took a slow sip of her coffee, exhaling as if gathering her thoughts. "I really enjoyed myself last night," she admitted, her voice calm but certain. "I enjoyed this morning too," she added quickly, flashing a small, playful smile. "But just to be clear," she continued, giving Rich a teasing look, "I enjoyed it... just not the taste."

Rich smirked while Chloe let out a small laugh, shaking her head as she flipped the eggs.

"Seriously," Beth went on, scrunching her nose, "I don't know how some women do it. I mean, I get it—it's the power in the moment—but it's definitely an acquired taste."

Rich chuckled. "I'll try to work on that for you."

Chloe snorted. "Yeah, good luck with that."

Steve, still trying to process his wife's surprisingly casual attitude about it all, cleared his throat. "So... does that mean you wouldn't do it again?" he asked hesitantly.

Beth pursed her lips, considering the question. "Hmm. I don't know." She turned to Rich, her expression unreadable but playful. "I wouldn't rule it out... but right now, I'm just not sure."

Steve's stomach did an odd little flip. The fact that she wasn't outright saying no sent an uncomfortable twinge through him.

Beth must have sensed his unease because she squeezed his hand and glanced at him with an almost amused expression. "Relax, honey," she murmured. "I think we both have a lot to process."

Steve nodded, exhaling slowly.

But before the conversation could move on, Beth suddenly tilted her head, as if something had just occurred to her. "You know what's really funny?" she mused. "I haven't given morning head in years. Not for you, not for anyone. And yet..." She trailed off, giving Rich a meaningful glance.

Steve felt his chest tighten.

Chloe let out a low whistle. "Damn, Beth. You just keep throwing those punches, huh?"

Beth shrugged, grinning as she took another sip of coffee. "Just saying. It's been a while."

Steve tried to ignore the way his stomach twisted. It wasn't just the act—it was what it meant. Something had changed in Beth, and he wasn't sure how far that change would go.

And whether or not that was a good thing... he wasn't quite sure yet.

Steve opened his mouth, hesitating. "I don't know if I'm sure about any of this—"

Before he could finish, Chloe sauntered over from the stove, still wearing nothing but her apron. Without hesitation, she reached down and wrapped her hand around his rock-hard cock, giving it a slow, teasing stroke.

"Really?" she murmured, tilting her head as she gazed up at him. "Because this says otherwise."

Steve inhaled sharply, his body betraying him yet again. Before he could respond, Chloe leaned in, pressing her lips against his in a slow, lingering kiss. She tasted like coffee, like warmth, like something effortless and confident, the opposite of the turmoil twisting inside him.

When she pulled away, she grinned. "Come on, Steve. Just admit it."

His jaw tightened, but the words tumbled out before he could stop them. "Beth enjoying herself turned me on."

Chloe giggled, her fingers tightening around him for just a second before releasing him. She turned to Beth with a knowing smirk. "See? I told you," she said playfully.

Steve frowned slightly. "Told her what?"

Chloe gave his chest a light tap. "That deep down, you've got that same submissive streak I found in Rich."

Beth laughed softly into her coffee cup, while Rich just chuckled from across the table.

Steve didn't argue. Because maybe, just maybe... Chloe was right.

Chloe let go of Steve's cock, stepping away from him with a playful smirk before turning her attention to Beth. With slow, deliberate movements, she approached her, her bare feet making no sound against the kitchen floor. Beth sipped her coffee, feigning nonchalance, but there was no missing the way her breath hitched slightly when Chloe reached out and slid her hands over her bare hips.

Beth stiffened, just for a moment, as Chloe's fingers traced over the curve of her ass, squeezing lightly.

"If what I did last night was out of line, honey, I apologize," Chloe murmured, her voice husky and low. She leaned in, her lips close to Beth's ear, her fingers still caressing her skin. "I just couldn't help myself."

Beth exhaled shakily, her grip tightening around her coffee cup.

"Oh no," she said quickly, almost too quickly. "I loved what you did to me, Chloe." Her voice softened as she continued. "I haven't had any experience with another woman before, but it was... incredible. Really incredible."

Chloe's lips curled into a knowing smile as her hands continued their slow exploration, sliding up Beth's waist and back down to cup the fullness of her ass. Beth shivered but didn't move away.

"I'm not a lesbian," Beth added hurriedly, as if needing to clarify it for herself more than anyone else.

Chloe chuckled, pressing a soft, teasing kiss to Beth's shoulder. "I didn't say you were," she murmured. "But you didn't stop me, either."

Beth swallowed hard, heat creeping up her neck. Behind them, the men watched with rapt attention, their coffee mugs momentarily forgotten.

"Amen, sister," Rich quipped. "You two were hot, and I do mean hot!"

Beth laughed, shaking her head. "Next time," she said, her voice quieter now, more thoughtful. "I think I need to return the favor, Chloe."

Chloe pulled back slightly, tilting her head as she studied Beth's face. "Do you?" she teased, trailing a single fingertip up Beth's spine.

Beth bit her lip, hesitating, but then she nodded, just once. "Yeah... I think I might."

Chloe grinned wickedly. "Good girl."

Rich leaned back in his chair, watching them with amusement. "I wonder how all this would be with an audience?" he mused aloud. "You know, the club is open again tonight. Maybe Steve and I would like to show our hot wives to a bunch of others and let them witness how well four friends can play give and take."

Beth, still flustered from Chloe's touch, blurted out, "I don't have another dress with me."

Chloe chuckled. "You can wear the same dress, honey, because you won't have it on long anyway." She turned toward Steve. "What do you think?"

Steve smirked, glancing at Beth, who was still catching her breath. "I'm game if Beth wants to go back tonight. I think we might end up spending most of our time upstairs if we do."

Beth let out a small laugh, shaking her head as if she still couldn't believe any of this was happening. "What can we do in the meantime?" she asked. "We've got the rest of the day."

"Well, Steve owes me one, but that can wait," Chloe chuckled, winking at him. "Beth, why don't you and I go out and find you a sexy new dress for tonight? The guys can clean up the beds and fix a late lunch. We can spend some time in the hot tub this afternoon but save ourselves for more adult fun tonight."

Steve's serious expression quickly turned into a smile. "Sounds like a plan," he remarked, showing that he was more than willing to allow his newly blossomed wife to explore even further. They still had a couple of days left of their visit, and if the past twenty-four hours were anything to go by... it was going to be one hell of a weekend.

THE RETURN VISIT

The club was already alive with energy when the two couples stepped inside. Music pulsed through the dimly lit space, a rhythmic thrum that vibrated in their chests. The dance floor was packed with couples moving in sync to the heavy bass, bodies pressing together under the glow of neon lights. The bar was just as lively, glasses clinking as bartenders poured drinks, laughter and conversation weaving through the charged air.

Heads turned as Chloe and Beth made their way through the crowd, heels clicking against the glossy floor. Eyes lingered, drawn in by the confidence in their steps, the way their dresses hugged their bodies like second skin. They found a table near the gleaming chrome pole where Beth had been the center of attention the night before.

Beth had chosen a short, red dress, bold and sultry. The strappy top crisscrossed over her breasts before tying at the back of her neck, leaving most of her back exposed. The thin, silky fabric draped over her curves, shifting with every movement, easily revealing the absence of any undergarments beneath.

Beside her, Chloe exuded effortless seduction in a classic black cocktail dress, its hemline daringly short—so short that every step threatened to expose more. The scoop neckline dipped low, the thin, delicate straps barely keeping it in place. The dress was simple, yet devastating, the kind that turned heads and made men ache to see what lay beneath.

As they reached their table, a few men cast lingering glances, some whispering, some openly admiring. The attention was electric, a reminder that tonight was still unwritten, still filled with possibilities.

Beth smoothed her dress as she sat, crossing her legs as she looked toward the stage. The pole gleamed under the lights, a silent invitation, a reminder of how easily she had lost herself in the moment the night before.

Chloe leaned in, her voice a sultry tease. "Nervous?"

Beth glanced at her, then at Steve and Rich, who were already watching them with interest. A slow, knowing smile curled her lips.

"Not even a little."

By the time Rich and Steve arrived at the table with drinks, both wives were already on the dance floor, moving in sync with new partners who had quickly seized the opportunity. The energy of the club pulsed around them, neon lights flashing as bodies swayed to the seductive rhythm of the music.

Beth was pressed against a tanned, muscular man with curly black hair and a well-groomed beard. His strong hands rested low on her hips, his grip firm but exploratory. She felt his palm drift lower, grazing over the curve of her unencumbered ass, his fingertips teasing against bare skin. The heat of his body enveloped her, his hard muscles shifting beneath her touch as she ran her fingers over his back. Then she felt it—the unmistakable swell growing against her thigh.

She wasn't surprised.

The music ended, and Beth gracefully pulled away, flashing her partner a polite but distant smile before making her way back to the table. She could feel his presence behind her, following, lingering with hopeful anticipation. But as soon as Steve and Rich rose to greet her, the man hesitated, his confidence faltering. Without a word, he turned and disappeared back into the crowd.

"Looks like you two drew a crowd," Rich chuckled, setting down the drinks. "Where's Chloe?"

Beth smirked, smoothing out her dress as she sat down. "He didn't waste any time," she said, nodding toward the dance floor. "He asked me to dance the moment we sat down. I think he was disappointed when he saw I was with you." She paused, then added with a small, playful shrug, "I didn't even ask his name."

Rich took a sip of his drink, his expression thoughtful. "It's likely we'll run into him again," he mused. "I'd be surprised if he gives up that easily."

Just then, Chloe returned from the dance floor, her hand wrapped around the wrist of a tall, blonde-haired man who followed her with a confident smile. She led him to the table with a casual ease, as if she had known him far longer than just a few songs.

"George," she said smoothly, giving his hand a light squeeze before releasing him. "Say hello to my husband, Rich, and our friends, Steve and Beth."

George nodded in greeting, his bright blue eyes scanning the group with a relaxed, knowing air.

Beth exchanged a quick glance with Steve, already sensing that tonight was about to get even more interesting.

Steve couldn't help but notice the sizeable bulge in George's slacks as the man returned to the table with Chloe. He smirked slightly, realizing that George had clearly enjoyed dancing with her. The man carried himself with ease, exuding quiet confidence, his hand resting lightly on Chloe's lower back as she slid into her seat beside Rich.

The two couples took to the dance floor for several songs, the pulsing beat of the music keeping the energy high. Between numbers, they returned to their drinks, laughing and exchanging knowing glances before slipping back into each other's arms. Partners shifted fluidly—Beth danced with Steve, then Rich, and eventually even with George. Chloe did the same, though Steve noticed that George seemed particularly eager to steal her away from Rich. Twice, he cut in before the song had even finished, guiding Chloe into another sultry rhythm without hesitation.

Steve watched the way Chloe responded, the way her body melted against George's, how her fingers lingered against his chest when she laughed at something he whispered in her ear. It was playful, but it was also undeniable that there was a real attraction there. Rich didn't seem bothered—if anything, he seemed to enjoy watching his wife be the center of someone else's attention.

After a few more dances, Beth took Steve's hand and led him back to their table, her skin warm from exertion, her breath slightly ragged. She picked up her drink and took a long sip before turning to him with a coy smile.

"This is quite a lively place," she said, her fingers tracing the rim of her glass. She tilted her head, her eyes searching his. "I hope you're enjoying yourself, honey."

Steve smiled, leaning in slightly. "I am. And I must say, you look stunning in that dress. You make me hard just looking at you, and I know I'm not the only one."

Beth smirked, her fingers grazing over his thigh beneath the table. "You mean muscle man?" she teased. "We only danced together once, and he was a bit pushy. Kept pressing his hard bulge right up against my leg. Not exactly subtle." She giggled, shaking her head.

Steve's jaw tightened slightly. He took a sip of his drink before responding. "I don't mind if he watches," he said, his voice measured, "but I think we should keep the playing between the four of us. Just to be safe."

Beth arched an eyebrow, leaning closer. "Steve, I think you're jealous," she teased, the corners of her lips curling up.

Steve exhaled, looking away for a moment before nodding. "Maybe a little," he admitted. "But we know Rich and Chloe. We don't know anything about all these other people. I'm just trying to be cautious."

Beth studied him for a moment, then nodded. "Okay. I'll tell Chloe and Rich that we're not comfortable playing with other people, and that dancing is our limit with them."

Before Steve could respond, Rich appeared beside them, his hand resting lightly on Beth's shoulder. "Limit?" he asked, his tone playful but curious. "Did I hear you say limit?"

Beth turned slightly, giving him a knowing look. "I just meant that Steve and I talked about it, and we'd prefer to keep things between the four of us. Dancing is fine, but beyond that, we'd rather keep it in the circle."

Rich nodded, his expression unreadable for a moment, then he smiled. "Fair enough. It's always best when everyone's comfortable."

Chloe returned just in time to hear the exchange, slipping into the seat beside Rich. She took a sip of her drink and glanced between Beth and Steve. "So, you two are keeping it in the family, huh?" she asked with a smirk.

Beth shrugged. "At least for now."

Chloe nodded, twirling the stem of her glass between her fingers. "Makes sense. No need to rush into anything. And besides..." She leaned in toward Beth, her voice dropping to a playful whisper. "You haven't even returned the favor yet."

Beth's cheeks flushed slightly, but she held Chloe's gaze, the flicker of something unspoken passing between them.

Steve shifted in his seat, watching the interaction, his mind racing with possibilities.

Rich leaned back in his chair, his lips curling into a sly smile as he met Beth's gaze. "Does that mean you'd like to go upstairs with Chloe and me pretty soon, Beth?" His voice was casual, but the heat in his eyes betrayed his intent.

Beth smirked, tilting her head playfully. "Either that or another drink," she quipped, taking a slow sip from her glass before setting it down with a deliberate motion.

Steve chuckled, pushing his chair back and stretching slightly. "I think we need to work off the drinks we've already consumed. Maybe we should check out one of those mirrored rooms again."

Chloe's eyes gleamed with excitement. "Is everybody ready to take a peek upstairs?"

The group exchanged glances before rising in unison. Steve noticed the anticipation in Beth's posture, the way her fingers lightly traced the rim of her glass before she turned to follow Rich and Chloe. He also noticed something else—movement from across the room.

George, still lingering nearby, subtly shifted toward the stairway. And just behind him, Beth's earlier dance partner—the muscular, tanned man who had pressed his body against hers—also began making his way toward the stairs, keeping a discreet distance.

Steve's jaw tightened slightly as he watched them maneuver through the crowd, keeping their interest veiled beneath the dim club lighting. It wasn't aggressive, but it was clear: they were following.

His eyes flicked back to Beth. She was completely unaware, laughing softly as she walked alongside Chloe, her slinky red dress swaying with every step. The fabric clung to her body, barely skimming her thighs, teasing glimpses of smooth, exposed skin as she moved.

Steve swallowed, feeling his cock stir as a rush of conflicting emotions flooded him. Excitement. Curiosity. A twinge of possessiveness. He didn't know what was about to happen, but the night was far from over.

Rich led the way as they ascended the staircase, the bass of the music from below muffling slightly as they moved toward the more intimate upper level of the club. The lighting was lower here, softer, casting deep shadows against the walls. The air was charged with anticipation.

"Let's take a look in the first room," Rich suggested, gesturing toward a darkened entryway.

They stepped inside the one-way mirror area, the room alive with movement and soft murmurs of pleasure. Couples and small groups were scattered across the space, tangled in various stages of intimacy. The four of them stood close together, taking in the scene, the atmosphere thick with raw energy.

Steve could feel Beth's warmth beside him, the slight hitch in her breath as she observed the display before them. He knew she was aroused. He could feel it—the way her body subtly leaned toward his, the faint shift of her thighs.

Then, over Beth's shoulder, he caught a glimpse of George and the muscular dancer stepping into the room behind them.

The game was changing.

As the four of them stepped into the mirrored room, Beth expected to be overwhelmed by the usual flurry of naked bodies and tangled limbs, but instead, her eyes were drawn to a single scene unfolding in the center of the room.

There was just one couple—but they commanded the entire space.

At the heart of the display stood a short, curvy brunette, naked and utterly uninhibited. She had long, dark hair that cascaded down her back, framing her soft, round face. Her features were delicate, naturally pretty, but what truly set her apart was the way she carried herself.

She was thick and soft, with generous curves that commanded attention. Her body carried extra weight—a plush belly, full thighs, and a wide, inviting ass—but she wore it with effortless confidence. Her big, natural breasts hung slightly with their own weight, and a dark patch of hair nestled between her thighs, unapologetically untouched.

Despite her softer frame, there was something about her—something magnetic. She didn't try to hide anything, didn't shrink herself. She owned her body, standing tall and proud, exuding a raw sensuality that made it impossible to look away.

Beth's gaze drifted slightly, and her breath hitched when she saw the man tied to the chair.

He was gorgeous—the kind of man who would turn heads on the street. Tall, blonde, sculpted, flawless. Even with his wrists bound behind the back of the chair and his muscular legs spread wide, there was no humiliation in his posture. He sat there on display, entirely exposed, his chiseled chest rising and falling steadily as he watched the woman with unwavering devotion.

Beth's eyes dipped lower, and she almost gasped aloud.

His cock was enormous.

Easily eight inches long, but it was the thickness that truly made her mouth go dry. His shaft was heavy and thick, the swollen head still nearly completely covered by his foreskin. Even as he sat motionless, his cock stuck out proudly from his body, its sheer girth making her pulse quicken.

Beth had always thought Rich was long. But this... this was something else entirely.

She barely registered when the three average-looking men surrounding the woman began their slow, methodical worship.

Beth watched, spellbound, as the first man kissed along the woman's thick neck, his lips trailing down her soft shoulder. Another man, standing behind her, ran his hands over her wide hips, kneading her flesh as he pressed soft, teasing kisses into the curve of her shoulder blade. The third man cupped her full, hanging breasts, palming them gently before his lips closed over one of her thick nipples.

She sighed contentedly, tilting her head back, completely unbothered by the way their hands roamed over her body, their cocks stiffening in response to her uninhibited pleasure.

Beth couldn't look away.

How? How did this woman—with a fat ass, a belly, and an unshaven pussy—have so much power?

Beth had never seen anything like it. She was in total control, letting herself be worshipped, her face glowing with satisfaction. She didn't just accept her body. She celebrated it.

And yet... her husband sat there, watching. Tied up. Waiting.

Beth's breath hitched as Chloe leaned in close, whispering against her ear.

"That's Jessie," Chloe murmured, her lips barely moving. "She's a regular here. And that gorgeous, thick-dicked man over there? That's Luke—her husband."

Beth swallowed, barely able to nod.

"He's a multi-millionaire," Chloe continued. "But a few years ago, Jessie figured out something about him. She discovered his inner submissive. And since then? Well, this is what they do. They come here every now and then, and she puts on a show."

Beth licked her lips, her voice barely above a whisper. "A show?"

Chloe smirked. "Oh, honey. This is just the warm-up."

Beth turned back, watching as the woman moaned softly, encouraging the men to explore further. One of them had slid his hand between her legs, his fingers parting the dense hair to stroke her, his other hand gripping the soft flesh of her ass.

Beth clenched her thighs together. She shouldn't be this turned on.

"And after this?" Chloe continued. "She's gonna suck and fuck each of them. One after the other. And Luke?" She nodded toward Jessie's incredibly well-endowed husband. "He'll sit right there and watch the whole thing. And when she's finished, they'll step outside so she can have a cigarette."

Beth blinked in confusion. "And... and then what?"

Chloe's smirk widened.

"Then, Luke will lick her ass while she smokes."

Beth's stomach fluttered uncontrollably. She turned to Chloe, trying to wrap her mind around the words she'd just heard. "Wait. You're telling me that he—" she glanced back at Luke's massive cock, still resting heavily against his thigh "—just lets her be with other men? Even when he looks like... that?"

Chloe giggled, running a finger over Beth's bare shoulder. "Oh, honey. You do get it. You just don't realize it yet."

Beth frowned. "I don't think I do."

Chloe turned toward her, mischief in her eyes. "Really?" she asked, dragging out the word. "Then tell me, Beth. Why did you swallow Rich's cum this morning when you hate the taste?"

Beth froze.

The realization slammed into her like a freight train.

She had done it. She had hated the taste. But in that moment... it wasn't about the taste.

Beth parted her lips, exhaling as the answer suddenly became painfully, beautifully obvious.

It was about power.

The power she'd had over Rich. The way she'd controlled the moment, the way she had taken something from him and claimed it as her own.

And as she turned back to Jessie—radiant, indulgent, dripping with sexual confidence as three men worshipped her soft, curvy body—Beth realized something else.

She wasn't disgusted.

She was fascinated.

And she was aching, undeniably wet.

"Let's check the other room," Chloe urged, her voice light but insistent. "This one's already getting crowded. Jessie always draws a crowd."

Beth's heart was still racing as she tore her gaze away from the scene. She felt a lingering heat between her legs, a deep, restless ache that hadn't been there before. As Steve and Rich stepped back, the mysterious hand that had brushed over her thigh quickly disappeared, leaving her aroused yet unsatisfied.

Without another word, the two couples slipped out of the mirrored room, moving toward the next doorway. This one was quieter, more intimate.

Inside, there was only one other couple—an older man and woman.

They lay on their sides, facing each other, their legs entwined in a slow, rhythmic motion. The woman's large, pendulous breasts swayed gently with each thrust, her soft body pressing against her husband's as he took his time, their connection slow and deliberate. Their eyes were locked, lost in each other as if no one else in the world existed.

Beth swallowed, feeling an unexpected warmth bloom in her chest. There was something deeply sensual about the way they moved, unhurried and completely attuned to each other. It was different from the raw exhibitionism in the other room, but in its own way, just as intimate.

"Want to use this room?" Chloe asked, a teasing lilt in her voice. "I think it's time we had some fun ourselves."

Beth exhaled slowly, still feeling the tingling remnants of

arousal from before. "Yes. Why not?" she agreed, her voice breathy.

Rich stepped forward, pushing the door open. The couple on the mattress looked up, meeting their eyes with wordless smiles before returning their attention to each other, undisturbed. The room was well-lit, warm, the air heavy with a heady mix of arousal and anticipation.

Beth stood in the center of the room with Chloe, glancing toward her friend. "What do we do?" she asked softly, suddenly feeling a rush of nervous excitement.

Chloe turned to her with a wicked grin. "First, we get naked," she giggled, already reaching for the straps of her barely-there dress. "Then, I want to see if I can get Steve hard before you can stiffen Rich's long cock."

Beth's breath hitched, her pulse quickening at the challenge.

Rich looked over at Steve, raising an amused eyebrow. "Sounds like an interesting contest, doesn't it?"

Steve let out a small chuckle, shaking his head. "I guess we'll find out."

Beth felt a surge of adrenaline as Chloe's dress slipped off her shoulders, pooling at her feet. This was happening. The game had officially begun.

In a moment, shoes, dresses, shirts, and slacks were tossed into a tangled pile, discarded without hesitation as the four of them gave in to their mutual hunger. The room was warm, the air thick with anticipation and the scent of arousal. Bare skin pressed against bare skin, fingers explored, mouths seeking, bodies giving in to the charged atmosphere.

Chloe was the first to act, scooting onto her knees in front of Steve. She reached for his hardening cock, wrapping her delicate fingers around his length and giving a teasing stroke. She glanced up, her lips parting slightly as she met his gaze with an unmistakable look of mischief. Without breaking eye contact, she leaned forward, her tongue flicking over his swollen tip before she slid his entire length into her mouth with practiced ease.

Steve gasped, his hands instinctively moving to Chloe's blonde hair as he felt the slick warmth of her throat surround him. She took him deep—so deep that her nose pressed against the patch of dark hair at the base of his shaft. He could feel the flex of her throat muscles as she held him there, her breath warm against his skin. Then, slowly, she pulled back, her lips dragging along every inch of him, leaving a wet sheen in her wake before plunging back down again.

Meanwhile, Rich had sprawled onto the soft mat, legs spread in obvious invitation. Beth crawled toward him, her body still buzzing with arousal from earlier. As soon as she was within reach, Rich pulled her into his embrace, his long arms wrapping around her as he guided her close. His mouth captured hers in a deep, lingering kiss, his tongue teasing hers while his hands explored her body.

Steve watched, mesmerized, as Rich's hands moved over Beth's soft breasts, kneading them before sliding down her sides. His fingers gripped her ass, spreading her slightly, exposing her to his touch. Beth moaned against his lips, her legs parting on their own, inviting him deeper into her most sensitive places.

Chloe, still kneeling in front of Steve, suddenly pulled off his cock with an audible pop, a thin string of saliva connecting her lips to his tip. She grinned up at him before lowering her mouth to his heavy balls. Her warm, wet tongue traced over his sensitive skin before she took one into her mouth, sucking gently as her fingers continued stroking his rigid shaft.

Steve groaned, his head tipping back as Chloe alternated between his balls, rolling them on her tongue, gently tugging his sack while stroking him with steady, deliberate movements. When he looked down, she was staring up at him with one eye, the other hidden behind the curve of his cock. The sight sent a deep pulse of pleasure through his body.

Across from them, Rich broke the kiss with Beth and whispered against her lips, "Suck it for me."

Beth met his gaze, her arousal surging. She slid down his body, her hands smoothing over his toned stomach as she positioned herself between his legs. She reached for his cock, long and firm, feeling the weight of it in her palm. She licked her lips, then ran her tongue along his shaft, tracing a slow, wet path from the base to the tip.

Rich groaned softly, his fingers tangling in Beth's hair as she kissed the broad head of his cock several times. Her tongue flicked over the slit, tasting him, before she slowly parted her lips and took him into her mouth.

She found a rhythm, her lips gliding smoothly over his length, her tongue swirling around the shaft as she worked him steadily. Her fingers curled around the base, stroking lightly as she sucked, enjoying the slow, sensual act.

Then she glanced over at Chloe.

Beth's breath caught slightly as she saw Chloe take Steve deep again, his entire length disappearing past her lips. She moved with practiced confidence, her throat working around him as Steve groaned, gripping her hair.

A spark of determination flared inside Beth.

She wanted to do that too.

She adjusted her angle, opening her mouth wider as she tried to take more of Rich's length. The first few extra inches went down smoothly, but as she pressed forward, the head of his cock nudged against the back of her throat. She gagged, pulling back instinctively.

Rich chuckled, his thumb stroking her cheek. "Take your time, baby," he murmured, his voice thick with arousal.

Determined, Beth licked her lips and tried again. This time, she relaxed her throat, breathing through her nose as she took him deeper. The pressure was intense, but she felt a small thrill when she managed to take more than before. She swallowed around him, earning a deep groan from Rich as his fingers tightened slightly in her hair.

Meanwhile, Chloe had resumed her rhythm on Steve, alternating between taking him deep into her throat and teasing his tip with her tongue. She hollowed her cheeks, creating a powerful suction that had Steve gripping her shoulders, his body tense with pleasure.

Beth, watching her, felt another rush of arousal. She wanted to go even further.

She steadied herself, then pushed forward once more, taking Rich as deep as she could. The stretch was intense, her throat tightening around him as she fought against the reflex. She held there for a moment before pulling back, gasping softly as she caught her breath.

Rich groaned, his grip tightening. "Damn, Beth," he muttered.

Encouraged, she did it again.

Steve, watching the two of them, felt his cock pulse in Chloe's mouth. The sight of his wife, her lips stretched around another man's cock, her throat working to take him in—he had never imagined it would arouse him like this.

Beth, feeling Rich twitch on her tongue, redoubled her efforts, wanting to push him further, wanting to take control of the moment.

And from the way he groaned her name, she knew she was succeeding.

"Holy fuck, I really didn't think I could suck it all," Beth panted, wiping a thin trail of saliva from her lips as she looked up at Rich. Her chest rose and fell with each breath, her arousal only intensifying. "It's too long."

"You did just fine," Rich assured her, his fingers brushing through her hair, his expression dark with desire. "Now, let's see how much you can take inside you, okay?"

Beth's eyes flickered with excitement as she nodded. "I'm so wet right now," she murmured, sliding her fingers down between her legs, confirming what she already knew. "I think I can take it all."

Straddling Rich's hips, she positioned herself above him, her thighs spreading wide as she reached between them to grasp his hard cock. The heat of it throbbed against her palm, slick with her own saliva. She tilted it upward, aligning it with her entrance.

Then she saw herself.

The full-length mirror on the wall captured everything—her naked, aroused body poised over another man's cock, her parted lips, her flushed cheeks, her erect nipples standing proud. Her legs were spread wide, her thighs trembling in anticipation. The glistening head of Rich's cock rested just against her soaked slit, teasing her entrance.

Beth's breath caught in her throat.

They could see her.

Anyone watching could see everything—her husband, the way he stood only a few feet away, watching his wife prepare to take another man. The two unknown men lingering near the doorway, silent spectators, their eyes locked onto the scene unfolding before them.

Oh, my God. I'm completely naked, and people are watching as I'm about to put Rich's hard cock inside me. Those two guys are probably watching me fuck my friend's husband.

A surge of heat tore through her, so intense that it nearly made her come before she even felt Rich inside her.

Biting her lip, she adjusted her grip, pressing his tip against her slick folds, rubbing it up and down over her entrance. Each stroke sent a fresh shiver through her, teasing herself as much as him. She circled her clit with his swollen head, using him to spread her own wetness before finally, finally, she allowed the broad tip to slip between her lips.

A low, drawn-out moan escaped her as she relaxed, letting the first few inches sink into her waiting heat.

Rich groaned beneath her, his hands gripping her hips as he resisted the urge to thrust up into her tight warmth.

"Fuck, Beth," he murmured, his voice thick with lust.

Beth was barely listening. The idea that other people were watching her take him, watching her stretch around his cock, created an urgent need deep in her belly. She needed more.

She pushed down, letting him slide deeper, her body stretching to accommodate his length. The sensation was overwhelming, but she wanted it all.

With a slow, deliberate movement, she lowered herself completely, her slick walls enveloping him until she felt the press of his pelvis against her own, his cock fully sheathed inside her.

A rush of pleasure bloomed in her core as she exhaled sharply.

"Ahh, yes," Rich groaned, his fingers tightening on her hips as he felt her take every inch of him.

Beth stared at herself in the mirror, transfixed. She could see everything—the way her thighs trembled as she settled onto him, the way her own reflection showed her completely full, her swollen lips stretched around the base of his cock.

The power of the moment hit her hard.

This was real.

And she loved it.

She rocked her hips experimentally, feeling the incredible sensation of his long shaft gliding inside her. A gasp left her lips as she started moving, finding her rhythm, her body responding instinctively to the pleasure.

"Fuck me, Beth," Rich growled, thrusting up slightly to meet her movements. "Fuck my big cock."

Beth shuddered, her fingers digging into his chest as she began to ride him in earnest, rolling her hips as waves of pleasure surged through her. The mirror reflected everything—her flushed skin, the erotic stretch of her body around him, the hungry way she took every inch.

And behind her, she could still see the two men watching, stroking themselves as they witnessed her surrender to pleasure.

Beth's body shivered as she found her rhythm, rolling her hips in long, slow movements over Rich's cock. His hands slid up to her breasts, thumbs flicking over her hard nipples as she rode him. Every time she lifted herself, his long shaft glistened, coated in her slickness, and every time she dropped back down, inch after inch of him disappeared once again into her wet heat.

Steve stood behind Chloe, his hands gripping her hips as he thrust into her from behind. His angle gave him an unobstructed view of everything—his wife's back to him, her spine arched, her hands braced on Rich's chest as she sank herself down onto another man's cock, again and again.

Beth's breath hitched as she became fully aware of the moment. She wasn't stretched—Rich's cock wasn't as thick as Steve's—but the length was unlike anything she had felt before. It filled her so completely, pressing into places she never realized could be reached.

She glanced up, her own reflection catching her eye for a moment in the full-length mirror.

She looked wrecked—her skin flushed, her lips parted, her breasts bouncing slightly with each movement. She could see herself riding Rich, see the way her body took him, and knowing she was being watched made her clench around him even tighter.

That's when her gaze shifted—and locked onto Chloe's.

Chloe was watching her.

Beth's lips curled slightly, her hips slowing for just a moment as she dragged her tongue across her bottom lip, a deliberate, teasing gesture meant only for Chloe to see.

Chloe's smirk deepened.

Steve groaned suddenly behind her, his grip on Chloe tightening as he thrust harder, the sight of his wife making him pulse inside Chloe's tight warmth.

"Harder, faster," Chloe urged Steve, her voice raw with need. "Fuck me and cum inside my hot cunt," she gasped. "I want to feel your warm juice all over inside me."

Beth whimpered at Chloe's words, her movements quickening as she rolled her hips more urgently, chasing her climax.

Steve grunted, slamming into Chloe's petite frame. The sights, the sounds—the wet slap of skin, the moans of both women—became too much.

He groaned loudly, grabbing Chloe's hips as his cock pulsed deep inside her, his release surging through him in thick, hot waves.

Beth felt herself teetering on the edge, the moment so intense, so completely overwhelming.

Rich's fingers tightened on her breasts, pulling at her nipples, heightening the pleasure even more.

Beth gasped, her head tipping back, her entire body locking up as the orgasm overtook her.

"Oh yes, yes, yes," Beth cried as her climax hit, pulsing around Rich's cock as waves of pleasure rolled through her.

Rich groaned beneath her, his hips lifting slightly, meeting her movements as he pushed as deep as he could go.

Beth felt it then—the sudden heat filling her completely, Rich's cock throbbing as he emptied himself inside her, groaning as he released deep into her womb.

She sat there for a moment, her body trembling, feeling completely, utterly full. Their combined juices began to leak from their joining, spilling onto Rich's crack, then onto the mat below.

Beth finally lifted her gaze—and found Chloe's eyes on her once more.

She licked her lips again, slower this time, holding her friend's gaze as she let the aftershocks of her climax roll through her.

Chloe smirked, tilting her head slightly.

Steve exhaled, still catching his breath, staring at his wife in a way he never had before.

And Beth—Beth knew she had crossed into something she could never take back.

Beth rolled off Rich, her limbs loose and heavy as she sprawled out on the mat. Her legs trembled from the effort, a deep, satisfied warmth still pulsing between them. She could feel the wetness trickling down the inside of her thigh, a stark reminder of just how thoroughly she'd been filled. Her chest rose and fell in deep, uneven breaths, the aftershocks of pleasure still making her toes curl.

She barely registered the soft brush of fingers against her skin until she felt the light pressure on her thigh.

Beth blinked lazily, turning her head to find Chloe sitting close beside her, one hand trailing up and down the curve of her leg, her nails grazing lightly over her still-sensitive skin. The blonde's lips were curled in a knowing smile, her eyes twinkling with mischief as she tilted her head.

"Was it good?" Chloe whispered, her fingers tracing slow, idle circles on Beth's inner thigh.

Beth stretched her arms above her head, letting out a contented sigh before smirking back at her friend. "Oh, yeah, it was marvelous," she replied, voice still thick with pleasure.

Chloe giggled softly, shifting closer until their bare legs were touching. "I could tell," she teased. "You looked like you were having the time of your life riding that long cock."

Beth chuckled, letting her head rest against the mat as she turned to face Chloe fully. "You were watching me, huh?"

Chloe's grin widened. "Oh, honey, I couldn't look away," she admitted, her fingers still tracing slow, lazy patterns over Beth's thigh. "I mean, the way you took him, so deep, so slow at first... and then, when you got really into it?" She exhaled dramatically, biting her bottom lip. "I think I might have gotten a little jealous."

Beth laughed, the warmth of Chloe's touch mixing with the residual pleasure still humming through her body. "Jealous?" she echoed, raising an eyebrow. "I don't believe that for a second. You had my husband fucking you hard right in front of me."

Chloe's nails dragged lightly up Beth's thigh, her fingers stopping just short of where the sticky aftermath of her pleasure remained. "Mmm, true," she mused, her eyes flickering down briefly before meeting Beth's gaze again. "But I think I was just as turned on watching you as I was from having Steve inside me."

Beth felt a fresh wave of heat creep up her neck at the blatant admission. Chloe was always bold, but something about the way she said it, the way her fingertips toyed at the edge of where Beth's legs met, made her stomach flutter in a way she wasn't used to.

"Is that so?" Beth mused, her voice playful but slightly breathless.

Chloe nodded, biting her lip again before dropping her gaze pointedly to Beth's chest. "You're still all flushed," she observed, her fingers now tracing over Beth's hipbone, teasing but not quite pushing further. "And look at these." She reached out, running a single fingertip over Beth's still-stiff nipple. "So sensitive... Are you sure you're done?"

Beth inhaled sharply, biting back a small gasp at the featherlight touch.

She turned onto her side, facing Chloe, their bodies just inches apart. "And what exactly are you suggesting?" she asked, arching an eyebrow.

Chloe grinned. "Oh, nothing," she said airily, dragging her fingertip slowly down between Beth's breasts, then lower, stopping just shy of her navel. "Just... curious."

Beth smirked, eyes flickering down briefly before locking back onto Chloe's. "Curious, huh?"

Chloe giggled again, leaning in slightly. "Mmmhmm," she hummed. "But only if you are."

Beth let the moment stretch, let the tension coil between them, playful and charged. Then, with deliberate slowness, she reached out, brushing a strand of blonde hair from Chloe's face before dragging her thumb lightly over her bottom lip.

"Maybe," Beth murmured, her own lips curling into a slow, teasing smile.

Chloe's eyes darkened slightly, but instead of pushing, she simply smirked. "I knew it," she whispered, her fingers giving Beth's thigh a final squeeze before pulling away.

Beth exhaled, half-relieved, half-disappointed.

Chloe just grinned at Beth for a second, her blue eyes gleaming with something darker, more intense. Then, without hesitation, her voice dropped, filled with raw hunger.

"I want to eat your pussy and make you cum again," she almost demanded.

Beth's breath caught in her throat. There was no teasing now, no playful build-up. Just raw, unfiltered desire.

Her gaze flickered toward Steve, who was now sitting up, watching them intently. His chest was still rising and falling from his release, his muscles taut with lingering tension. He wasn't just watching. He was waiting.

Then Beth turned her head slightly, looking at the mirrored wall. Her reflection met her gaze—her flushed skin, the faint tremble in her thighs, the visible evidence of what she had just done with Rich still leaking from her.

Something inside her tipped.

"Okay," she breathed.

Chloe wasted no time.

Sliding between Beth's open legs, she pressed her mouth against her friend's still-sensitive folds, her tongue darting out to taste what had been left behind.

Beth gasped, her body arching slightly as the first stroke of Chloe's tongue sent shivers down her spine. The warm wetness, the slow, deliberate suction—it was different from anything she had ever felt before.

She spread her legs wider, fully offering herself, moaning as Chloe's lips sealed around her, pulling everything from her with deep, sensual strokes.

Rich, watching the two women entwined in pleasure, felt a fresh surge of need. He shifted onto his knees, moving behind Chloe, running his hands over her back, down the curve of her hips. He could see her tongue working Beth, see the way Beth's slickness coated her lips. The sight made his own cock stir, already beginning to harden again despite the intensity of his last orgasm.

Leaning down, he gripped Chloe's ass, spreading her slightly, before lowering his mouth to her waiting heat.

The moment his tongue touched her, his body tensed. The mix of Steve's seed and Chloe's own arousal coated his tongue, and for a split second, his face contorted slightly. It wasn't a taste he enjoyed—but the sheer submission of the act, the knowledge of what he was doing, what it meant, sent a jolt of something dark and intoxicating through him.

Steve, watching closely, expected Rich to pull away, but instead, he doubled down.

Rich groaned against Chloe's folds, pressing his tongue deeper, the vibrations making Chloe moan loudly against Beth. As Steve's eyes flicked downward, he realized with shock that Rich's cock, so recently spent, was already beginning to harden again.

The arousal in submission—it was obvious.

And it was turning Rich on more than anything.

Steve was still processing it when he felt Beth's fingers wrap around him. Crawling over to his wife, he knelt close, offering her his limp member, and without hesitation, she took him into her mouth.

Beth's tongue swirled over his head, teasing the sensitive underside before drawing him deeper, her soft lips wrapping around him as she slowly, deliberately sucked him back to full hardness.

Steve groaned, his hands moving into her hair, watching as she devoured the very cock that had been inside Chloe just minutes before.

Around them, the club's voyeurs were far from passive.

George, the blonde-haired man who had danced with Chloe earlier, now stood with his cock out, long and glistening as the redheaded woman worked her mouth over him. She was on her knees, her fiery hair tumbling over her shoulders as she bobbed her head up and down his shaft, her lips stretching over his thick length.

Beside them, Beth's muscular dance partner groaned as a young brunette wife sucked his cock, her fingers wrapped tightly around the base. Her tongue traced the thick veins along his shaft before she plunged him deep into her throat, taking him with greedy enthusiasm.

The woman's husband stood just beside them, stroking himself with slow, deliberate strokes. His cock was long and thick, his grip tight as he watched his wife pleasure another man. His eyes were locked onto her lips, the way she moaned around the other man's length, the way her saliva coated him as she took him deeper.

The air was thick with the wet sounds of mouths working, soft moans, the heat of bodies fully lost in indulgence.

Chloe let out a sudden, muffled moan against Beth, her thighs trembling as Rich's tongue worked her relentlessly. Her breathing hitched, and then her whole body shuddered as her orgasm hit.

"Fuck—oh, fuck," Chloe gasped, her hands gripping Beth's thighs as her climax overtook her, sending hot pulses of pleasure through her core.

Seconds later, Beth cried out, her hips rolling against Chloe's mouth as her own release crashed over her.

Her whole body tensed, her fingers tightening around Steve's cock as wave after wave wracked her, her thighs squeezing around Chloe's face as she came hard.

And then, just like that, it was over.

Beth lay back for a moment, catching her breath, feeling the final tremors still moving through her. Chloe sat back, licking her lips slowly, her face slick with Beth's arousal.

Then the girls stood.

Steve and Rich remained kneeling, their cocks standing rock hard and neglected, both men looking up at the women who had just unraveled them.

Chloe smirked, exchanging a look with Beth before tilting her head.

"I think we're done for now," she teased, wiping the corner of her mouth with her thumb.

Beth chuckled, stretching her arms above her head, her body still thrumming with pleasure. "For now," she echoed, flashing Steve a playful glance before turning away deliberately.

Rich exhaled, running a hand through his hair as he looked down at his still-rigid cock, shaking his head with a breathless laugh.

Steve groaned, sitting back on his heels.

The girls walked away together, their hips swaying as they left both men aching, needing, and utterly at their mercy.

And from the way Chloe looked over her shoulder with that knowing grin, they both knew—

This wasn't over.

Not by a long shot.

THE MOMENT AFTER

Slowly, the two couples began to stir, slipping back into their clothes, the heat of their encounter still lingering in the air. The older couple, who had been watching the entire performance, finally rose and walked toward them—completely naked.

Beth's eyes traveled over them both as they approached.

The woman, blonde with a few streaks of gray running through her otherwise full hair, was in remarkable shape for her age. Her body was toned and fit, her waist still narrow, her hips carrying just enough softness to complement her athletic frame. Her breasts, though small and sagging, had a natural, effortless appeal, the way they swayed freely only adding to her mature beauty.

Her husband, Eric, was equally striking. Even in his early fifties, he still carried himself with the kind of confidence that only came with age and experience. He was broad-shouldered, tanned, with a dusting of salt-and-pepper hair on his chest. But what immediately caught Beth's eye was his cock—thick and hanging heavily between his legs, even soft. The foreskin covered most of his head, but the sheer girth of him was undeniable.

"That was incredible," the woman murmured, running a hand

down her husband's chest. "I got so wet, I could hardly feel Eric's cock until he shot his cum inside me. I kept remembering how much more energy we used to expend when we fucked with our friends. We haven't come together that hard in years!"

Eric chuckled, his deep voice warm as he turned his gaze toward Beth and Chloe. "You two gals really turned us on," he said, his soft but undeniably thick cock bobbing gently as he shifted his weight. His eyes twinkled with mischief. "May I just get one brief feel of your titties before you leave?"

Beth paused, her silky red dress draped over her arm. She glanced at Chloe, who only smirked.

"Make it quick," she replied, turning to face him.

Eric's hands, rough with age but firm, moved to her chest. He cupped Beth's soft breast carefully, weighing the full mound in his palm, his thumb circling over her still-sensitive nipple. His touch was surprisingly gentle, almost reverent, as if appreciating something truly special.

Chloe, grinning, took his other hand and placed it on her own smaller, perkier breast. "Don't forget about me," she teased.

Eric let out a low chuckle, his thumbs rolling over their nipples, feeling them stiffen further beneath his touch. As he did, Chloe's gaze dropped down to his impressive girth, still hanging heavily, and without hesitation, she reached out and wrapped her slim fingers around his thick shaft.

Beth's breath hitched as she watched Chloe pull at his foreskin, peeling it back slightly, revealing the smooth, swollen head underneath.

She had never been with an uncut man before.

Curious, she reached out tentatively, her fingers brushing over the exposed tip. "It's so different," she murmured, glancing at

Chloe. "I've never been with someone uncut before."

Chloe smirked, stroking Eric a little more firmly. "It's fun, isn't it? The way the skin moves... and how sensitive it makes them."

Eric groaned softly, his cock already beginning to swell in their hands, the soft flesh thickening beneath their touch.

Beth felt a strange thrill at the difference. She ran her fingers along the ridge of his foreskin, watching as it retracted slightly with her movements, then slid forward again as she released it. It was so unlike what she was used to, but the way Eric's cock responded so quickly to their touch was undeniably arousing.

Then, just as smoothly as she had engaged, Beth took a step back, grabbing Steve's hand and pulling him with her.

"Let's watch this one from the sidelines," she murmured.

Steve nodded, wrapping an arm around her waist as they stepped back to simply take in the scene.

Chloe, still kneeling in front of Eric, gave Beth one last playful glance before lowering her head.

She kissed the exposed head of his cock, teasing it with the softest brush of her lips before opening her mouth wide and taking him inside.

Eric groaned, his hands instinctively moving to Chloe's blonde hair, his fingers threading through the strands as she sucked him in deeper, her tongue swirling around the head before sliding down his shaft.

The wet, eager sound of her sucking filled the room, her enthusiasm unmistakable.

And that was all it took for Eric's wife to get involved.

Beth turned just in time to see the older blonde step toward Rich, running her hand across his firm chest, nails lightly scraping his skin as she trailed downward. Her fingers brushed against his stomach before wrapping around his already firm cock, stroking him slowly.

Then, without hesitation, she dropped to her knees.

Beth and Steve exchanged a glance, both equally entranced by the woman's confidence.

She took her time, teasing the tip of Rich's cock with her tongue, tracing small circles over the sensitive head before enveloping him in her mouth.

From the very first movement, it was obvious—she was experienced.

Her head moved with fluid precision, her lips stretching effortlessly around his length. She took him deeper, her throat relaxing as she swallowed more of him, her hand twisting at the base to meet each descent.

Rich groaned, his head tilting back as she worked him, her tongue dragging over every inch of him with the kind of skill only years of practice could perfect.

Beth felt a new rush of arousal at the sight.

She glanced at Chloe, watching her friend's soft lips stretch around Eric's thick cock, the way her fingers curled around the base, stroking the shaft in time with each bob of her head.

Eric was breathing heavily now, his cock fully erect, the foreskin gliding smoothly with each motion as Chloe's lips sealed tighter around him.

Meanwhile, his wife continued her expert assault on Rich, one hand fondling his heavy balls while the other gripped the base of his shaft, guiding him deeper and deeper into her mouth.

Steve's grip on Beth's waist tightened as he exhaled, watching the scene unfold.

"Looks like they're enjoying themselves," Beth murmured.

Steve let out a breathless chuckle. "Yeah… that's one way to put it."

They stood there, simply observing, both undeniably aroused by the way the older couple indulged in the moment so effortlessly.

Beth shifted slightly, pressing herself into Steve's side, feeling the heat radiating off of him.

Neither of them spoke, content to just watch.

For now.

As they waited in the dimly lit hallway, the tension still thick from what they had just witnessed, George and his redheaded companion joined them. Moments later, Beth's earlier dance partner, the muscular, tanned man, emerged as well, looking freshly satisfied but still carrying the same hungry energy from the club floor.

"That was the hottest thing I've ever witnessed," George gushed, shaking his head in disbelief. His girlfriend, Ellie, nodded eagerly beside him, her flushed cheeks and bright eyes betraying just how much she had enjoyed the scene.

"We're staying at a hotel just a mile from here," George continued, his tone dropping slightly, laced with an unspoken invitation. "Would you guys like to continue the party in our room?"

Steve hesitated. There was no doubt that the night had already pushed past the boundaries of what he had once imagined possible, but now? Moving to a hotel with virtual strangers? He shot a glance at Beth, trying to read her.

"We'll have to see what our friends want to do after they finish," he answered carefully, nodding toward the closed door. "We're their guests, so they should decide, I think."

Beth, however, was more intrigued than wary. She turned to the muscular man standing beside George. "I don't think we were properly introduced," she said with a small smile. "I'm Beth, and this is my husband, Steve. Are you with George?"

The man shook his head, a confident smirk tugging at his lips. "Nice to meet you, Beth. I'm Tommy. No, I'm not with George and Ellie," he clarified, glancing briefly at them.

"Uh, you're welcome to join us too, Tommy," George interjected quickly, the excitement in his voice evident. "We don't mind entertaining a single guy, do we, Ellie?"

Ellie, still clutching George's arm, gave a little shrug before nodding. "You're welcome to come along, Tommy," she said smoothly.

The conversation was interrupted as the door opened, and Rich and Chloe stepped into the hallway, both looking thoroughly satisfied. Chloe's lips were still slightly swollen, her blonde hair tousled from where Eric's hands had gripped it. Rich, for his part, seemed more composed, though there was a noticeable ease in his posture, the kind that only followed a truly mind-blowing release.

"Gee, looks like a convention out here," Rich quipped, his dark eyes flicking over the assembled group.

"George and Ellie have invited us to a party in their hotel room," Beth announced before Steve could even bring it up. Her voice was lighter than usual, almost eager. Steve turned to look at her, realizing in that moment she wanted this. She wanted to go.

Rich glanced over the group, weighing the decision. "Don't you gals want to stay for the dance contest?" he asked, raising a brow. "Beth or Chloe are sure to be big hits again."

"If the girls want to dance, we have music through the cable TV in our room," George countered smoothly. "They can really entertain us in private."

Ellie giggled at his words, pressing into his side, her fingers teasing along the waistband of his pants.

"I'm ready to strut my stuff for George," Chloe chimed in, her voice low, sultry. She tossed Rich a wink, letting her fingers trail over his arm before slipping back toward George's side.

Rich turned to Steve and Beth, waiting. "It's up to you guys," he said, his voice even. "Want to stay here, go to the hotel, or head home?"

Beth squeezed Steve's arm, her grip firmer than usual, her body language clear.

"I'm with Chloe," she answered before Steve could even process the weight of the choice. "At the hotel, we could dance and have some more fun. We have all day tomorrow at Rich and Chloe's house."

Steve's stomach twisted slightly. He had already seen so much tonight—Beth being filled in a way he never had, Beth teasing Chloe, Beth riding another man while he watched helplessly aroused. And now, this?

But as his gaze drifted over Ellie, a brief vision of her pink nipples and the soft curls of her ginger hair between her thighs flashed through his mind. The way she had expertly worked Rich's cock, her skill, her confidence.

He swallowed, his body betraying him even before his mind

could catch up.

"I guess we should let the girls show off a little more," he finally replied, forcing a chuckle.

Beth smiled at him, eyes gleaming, knowing full well what she had just done.

George grinned. "Then it's settled," he said, his voice brimming with excitement. "Let's get out of here."

The group turned toward the exit, the air thick with unspoken anticipation, new temptations, and the lingering heat of the night that had only just begun.

THE FINAL STEPS

George's hotel room turned out to be a spacious junior suite, complete with two large beds, a wet bar, and a living area filled with plush couches and chairs surrounding a massive plasma TV. It was the perfect setting for what was quickly shaping up to be an afterparty unlike any other.

George moved behind the bar, pouring drinks while Rich took control of the TV, flipping through channels until he landed on one playing energetic party music. Tommy helped distribute the drinks, passing out glasses as the men settled into their seats in the living area, their eyes already locked onto the unfolding scene before them.

Chloe, leading the charge, pulled Ellie and Beth toward the open space in front of the TV. The music pulsed through the room, a steady, insistent beat that vibrated through their bodies.

Beth swayed to the rhythm, loosening herself up, while Ellie, already feeling the energy, began to run her hands along her own body, her movements slow and teasing.

Then Chloe turned toward Ellie, a playful smirk on her lips, and reached out, brushing a strand of red hair from the other woman's cheek. Ellie leaned into the touch, and with the smallest of nods, Chloe leaned in, capturing her lips in a slow, deliberate kiss.

A murmur rippled through the room.

Steve watched, his pulse spiking, as Ellie responded eagerly, her hands sliding up Chloe's waist, fingers grazing the curve of her breast as their kiss deepened.

Beth, still moving to the beat, bit her lip as she watched them. There was something so effortless about the way they touched, the way Ellie melted into Chloe's kiss, her fingers kneading lightly over Chloe's soft, perky breasts.

Chloe was the first to shed her clothing. She kicked off her heels and, now barefoot, she let her hands slide over Ellie's hips before tugging at the hem of her blouse. Ellie lifted her arms, letting Chloe peel it away, revealing a nearly transparent lace bra beneath.

Ellie smirked, tossing her blouse aside before turning her back to Chloe, rolling her shoulders seductively as she let Chloe undo the clasp of her bra.

As the garment fell away, Steve sucked in a sharp breath.

Ellie's full, creamy white breasts spilled free, dusted with faint freckles. Her small, pink nipples were already firm, the slight chill of the room—or maybe the heat of the moment—making them stand at attention.

Ellie turned slowly, giving each man a full, deliberate view, her confidence evident in the way she held herself.

Chloe didn't let her stand alone for long. She pressed her bare chest against Ellie's back, her hands sliding forward, cupping Ellie's full breasts, thumbs brushing over her stiff nipples as she pressed a lingering kiss to Ellie's neck.

Ellie let out a soft moan, arching into Chloe's touch, tilting her head to the side to grant her more access.

"Goddamn," George muttered from his seat, eyes locked on the display.

Beth, still swaying to the music, watched with growing arousal but held off on joining in. Instead, she let herself enjoy the show, her hands moving idly over her own hips, feeling the thin fabric of her dress against her skin.

Chloe, now completely nude, continued exploring Ellie's body, her hands trailing lower as Ellie's breathing grew heavier.

Ellie finally stepped forward, turning to face Chloe fully, her hands sliding down the blonde's bare stomach before reaching the waistband of her own skirt. She pushed it down slowly, letting it slide over her hips, pooling at her feet.

A shiver ran through the room as she hooked her thumbs into her lacy panties, dragging them down her long, toned legs.

The moment they were off, she stepped back toward Chloe, pressing their bodies together once more, her soft, natural curves molding against Chloe's lithe frame.

Ellie's red bush was natural, neatly trimmed but full enough that Steve could see the glistening pink of her slit through the damp curls.

She moved toward Steve now, her bare skin illuminated by the warm lighting of the suite. Her hips swayed as she closed the distance, stopping just in front of him.

She locked eyes with him, a playful smirk tugging at her lips as she rolled her hips in slow, hypnotic movements.

For a moment, Steve forgot how to breathe.

Ellie reached for his hand, guiding it toward her hip,

encouraging him to touch her.

And he did.

His fingers traced her waist, trailing downward, feeling the contrast of her soft skin against the wiry curls below.

Chloe, watching with a knowing grin, moved behind Ellie once more, her hands gliding over Ellie's stomach, fingers brushing the underside of her breasts.

Rich and George sat transfixed, their drinks forgotten as they watched the women tease and explore each other with sensual confidence.

Beth exhaled, her own arousal mounting as she took in the scene.

She hadn't expected this.

And she couldn't look away.

Beth watched as her husband let his fingers slide along Ellie's slick, glistening slit. The redhead shivered under his touch, her hips rolling forward as she silently encouraged him to go further.

Steve hesitated for only a moment before slipping one thick finger inside her, feeling the warmth of her swollen pussy wrap around him. Ellie gasped, her head tilting back slightly, eyes fluttering closed as Steve curled his finger within her, testing her reactions.

Beth's pulse quickened.

The sight of her husband toying with Ellie, the way the other woman responded so eagerly, sent a spark through her—a mix of arousal, possessiveness, and the undeniable need to match what was unfolding before her.

With a breathless laugh, she seized the moment.

In one fluid motion, Beth pulled her red dress over her head and let it drop to the floor, leaving her completely exposed to George and Tommy.

The two men, who had until recently been little more than strangers—mere spectators behind a mirror—now had a front-row seat to her voluptuous curves, her soft, heavy breasts, and the undeniable heat between her thighs.

A thrill ran through her at the thought.

She cupped her hands beneath her full breasts, lifting them slightly, offering them up like a gift.

"Like what you see?" she teased, her voice dripping with confidence.

George was already stripped down, his cock thick and heavy in his hand as he slowly stroked himself, eyes locked on her every movement.

Tommy, realizing he was still clothed, hurried to catch up. He tugged off his shirt, revealing his sculpted chest, then quickly shed his pants and briefs, kicking them aside as he settled onto the couch beside George.

Beth smirked as she swayed closer to them, rolling her hips in slow, deliberate motions, her bare skin catching the dim light of the suite.

She glanced between the two men, feeling their eyes roam over her body, drinking her in.

Beth's attention shifted as she noticed Chloe moving toward George with deliberate intent.

With a sultry smirk, Chloe straddled him, settling her bare

thighs over his lap, her movements fluid and confident. George leaned back against the couch, his hands instinctively settling on her hips as she pressed her full, perky breast to his lips.

"Open up," she murmured, teasing him as she traced a finger along his jawline.

George obeyed, taking her stiff nipple into his mouth, his tongue circling the sensitive peak before sucking it between his lips. Chloe let out a soft sigh, arching her back slightly, her fingers threading into his short hair as she ground her hips against his lap.

Beth watched, mesmerized, as Chloe reached between them, wrapping her fingers around his cock. Even sitting down, George's size was impressive—his shaft long and thick, standing proudly against her palm.

She guided him to her entrance, teasing herself with the broad head, rolling her hips in slow circles as she slickened him with her arousal.

Then, with a slow, deliberate motion, she sank down.

A collective murmur rippled through the room as Chloe took him inch by inch, stretching around his girth, her body swallowing him deeply.

She let out a low, breathy moan as he filled her, her nails digging into his shoulders as she adjusted to the size of him.

Beth could hear it—the wet, sticky sounds of their joining, the unmistakable squelch of Chloe's soaked pussy molding around George's thick cock.

Soon, her movements became rhythmic, a slow back-and-forth grind that deepened with each motion. The soft smack of skin meeting skin filled the air, punctuated by Chloe's quiet moans and George's deep, approving groans.

Beth swallowed, feeling her own arousal pulse between her thighs as she watched Chloe lose herself in the moment.

Beth turned her attention to Tommy, studying him for a moment.

He was already sitting back on the couch, his legs slightly spread, his thick cock resting heavily against his thigh. Even soft, he looked wide, his girth undeniable, but it was the foreskin that made her hesitate.

She had never been with an uncut man before.

Something about it felt unfamiliar—the way the skin still covered the head, how different it looked compared to what she was used to. She bit her lip, contemplating whether to proceed.

Chloe, sensing her hesitation, leaned in close, brushing Beth's shoulder with her own as she whispered playfully, "You're going to love it, trust me. It's so much fun once you get the hang of it."

Beth glanced up at her friend, searching her face for reassurance. Chloe just smirked, her fingers running briefly over Tommy's thigh before giving Beth an encouraging nod.

"Just start slow," Chloe murmured. "Let the skin do some of the work for you."

Taking a deep breath, Beth placed a hand on each of Tommy's knees, feeling the heat of his skin beneath her palms as she slowly spread them apart, making room for herself.

As she lowered onto her haunches, she wrapped her fingers around his shaft, noting how different it felt—the extra give of the foreskin as she stroked him experimentally.

Tommy exhaled sharply, his cock twitching in response.

Encouraged, Beth curled her fingers around the base, gently

pulling the skin back, revealing the smooth, swollen head beneath. She watched as it emerged, the contrast striking, and for a moment, she simply admired the way it looked.

"You see?" Chloe cooed, her voice laced with amusement. "It's just like unwrapping a present."

Beth chuckled softly, shaking her head before lowering her lips to him.

The first touch of her tongue sent a shudder through Tommy's body. He groaned, his head tipping back against the couch as she licked tentatively, circling the newly exposed tip, testing how he responded.

His reaction was immediate—his thighs tensed, his breath hitched, and his fingers curled against the cushions beside him.

Feeling more confident, Beth wrapped her lips around him, sliding him into her mouth inch by inch, the girth making her jaw stretch as she adjusted.

She moved slowly at first, taking her time to explore him, letting her tongue glide over the sensitive underside as she stroked the base, her fingers experimenting with how the foreskin moved as she pumped him gently.

Chloe hummed approvingly. "See? You're a natural."

Tommy let out another low, guttural groan, his hips shifting slightly as Beth deepened her rhythm, finding a steady pace that had him breathing harder with each stroke.

She glanced up briefly, her lips still wrapped around his thick cock, just in time to see the pleasure etched across his face.

Then, curiosity getting the better of her, she let her hand do the work, stroking him in sync with the natural glide of the skin, watching how easily it moved, how the added sensation made his hips jerk beneath her touch.

It was fascinating—so different from what she was used to—but in a way that made her eager to master it.

By the time she had him fully hardened, his cock throbbing in her grasp, she popped him from her lips with a soft, wet sound, taking a moment to admire how flushed he had become.

Finally, she glanced over at Steve.

Her husband was watching her intently, his expression unreadable, but the bulge pressing against his pants told her everything she needed to know.

Beth smirked, wiping the corner of her mouth with the back of her hand before turning back to Tommy.

Now that she had figured out how to handle him, she wasn't quite finished yet.

As Beth focused on Tommy, feeling the weight of his thick cock in her hand, a shift in the atmosphere caught her attention.

Ellie had moved.

Rather than waiting for Steve to take her, she took control of the moment, positioning herself between him and Rich on the sofa. With an effortless confidence, she spread her legs slightly, settling comfortably between them as though she belonged there.

Steve and Rich, both still engrossed in watching their wives with other men, barely had time to react before Ellie reached out with both hands, wrapping her fingers around their cocks simultaneously.

A soft gasp escaped Steve's lips as he felt Ellie's firm but deliberate grip stroking him, her fingers expertly sliding up and down his shaft in slow, teasing motions.

Rich, who had been lounging beside her, inhaled sharply, his body tensing as her delicate fingers wrapped around him as well. Ellie gave him a playful squeeze, tilting her head toward him with an amused smirk.

"You like watching them, don't you?" she murmured, her voice low and sultry as her hands worked in tandem, stroking them both with an easy, rhythmic pace.

Neither man answered.

They didn't need to.

Their cocks, thickening under her touch, told her everything she needed to know.

Ellie chuckled softly, shifting slightly, adjusting her grip to pump them in slow, measured strokes. "I bet it drives you crazy," she mused, leaning in closer, her breath hot against Steve's ear. "Seeing Beth like that... taking another man inside her."

Steve swallowed hard, his hips instinctively pushing up into her touch, betraying any restraint he might have had.

Rich let out a quiet groan as Ellie's thumb swept over his swollen tip, smearing the bead of pre-cum that had gathered there.

"You're both so hard," she observed, her voice laced with amusement.

She tightened her grip slightly, alternating the pace between them, keeping them both right on the edge—just enough to tease, but not enough to let them tip over.

Steve gritted his teeth, his focus flickering between his wife, who was now spread open beneath Tommy, and the redheaded woman who now had him at her mercy.

Beth, oblivious to the shifting dynamic on the couch, looked up at Tommy from where she lay sprawled on the floor, her legs wide and inviting.

"Fuck me, Tommy," she gasped, her voice thick with need. "Fuck me now!"

Ellie chuckled softly, stroking both Steve and Rich just a little faster.

"Oh, this is going to be fun," she murmured, her lips curling into a knowing smirk.

And as Steve moaned under her grip, she knew she had both of them exactly where she wanted them.

Tommy scrambled onto the floor, his urgency evident as he positioned himself between Beth's open legs. His thick, eager cock twitched as he moved into place, his hand instinctively wrapping around the base to guide himself toward her soaked slit.

Beth watched, anticipation coiling in her belly as she saw his cock bob slightly, the swollen tip slick with his arousal.

Then she felt it—the first press of his head against her entrance.

There was a pause, a fleeting moment where she felt the difference immediately. Tommy wasn't as long as she was used to, but the sheer girth of him was undeniable.

A breath hitched in her throat as he pushed forward, the broad head stretching her in a way that sent a sharp jolt of pleasure rippling through her core.

Her body resisted for just a second, then yielded, welcoming him inch by inch as he filled her.

Beth gasped.

"Jesus, you're thick," she moaned, her hands gripping the carpet beneath her.

Tommy groaned, his jaw tightening as he pushed deeper, his cock stretching her walls wider than she was used to. What he lacked in length, he more than made up for in sheer fullness, his shaft pressing insistently against her most sensitive spots.

Then, he hit it—her G-spot.

The blunt head of his cock rubbed against it again and again, and Beth felt her body clench around him involuntarily.

A pulse of white-hot pleasure shot through her, her breath hitching as she rocked her hips upward, chasing the sensation.

Tommy, feeling her react, adjusted his movements, angling his strokes just right—massaging that perfect spot with every thrust.

Beth's orgasm came fast and hard, her body trembling as waves of pleasure crashed over her.

"Keep going, keep going!" she urged, her voice shaking as the aftershocks still pulsed through her core.

Tommy didn't need to be told twice.

Gripping her hips, he pumped into her fevered womb with renewed determination, each thrust deep and deliberate, his thickness stretching her wide with every plunge.

Beth's moans turned into breathless gasps, her body arching off the floor as she felt every inch of him grinding into her, filling her completely.

"I'm so full," she panted, her nails digging into his arms. "So full!"

Tommy growled in response, his pace quickening, their bodies moving together in a perfect, primal rhythm.

As the moans and wet, rhythmic sounds of sex filled the room, Ellie took center stage. She rose with deliberate grace, her body radiating dominance, and turned to face the two men sitting on the edge of the couch, their gazes torn between the sight of their wives being taken and the fire in her eyes.

"On your knees," she commanded, her voice sultry yet firm.

Rich obeyed instantly, eager, his breath shallow, his cock already throbbing with need. Steve hesitated, just for a beat, his eyes darting toward Beth, who was lost in the throes of raw pleasure beneath Tony. But the silent pressure of the moment, the unspoken expectation, had him lowering himself beside Rich, heart hammering against his ribs.

Ellie spread her legs, the thick, copper curls of her pussy glistening with arousal. She reached out, cupping Rich's chin, tilting his face up. "Lick me," she murmured, her voice a mixture of invitation and command.

Rich needed no further instruction. He leaned in, inhaling the intoxicating scent of her before pressing his mouth against her slick folds. His tongue worked eagerly, broad strokes at first, tasting her fully before honing in on the sensitive bud at the peak of her sex. Ellie let out a throaty moan, fingers tangling into his hair, guiding him exactly where she wanted him.

Behind her, Steve hovered in uncertainty, his breath warm against her skin, his lips inches from the delicate curve of her ass. He'd never done this before. The thought of it had never even crossed his mind. Yet here he was, kneeling behind this confident, dripping, radiant woman, about to cross a line he never thought he'd approach.

"Go on," Ellie purred, glancing over her shoulder, her eyes dark with lust. "Use your tongue."

His pulse pounded in his ears as he swallowed hard. Then, with a slow, tentative movement, he pressed his mouth against her, his tongue tracing along the curve of her rear, warm and wet. The first taste was unfamiliar, but the low, shuddering moan that slipped from Ellie's lips sent a rush of heat straight to his cock.

She liked it.

Emboldened, he parted her with his hands, his tongue working in slow, experimental circles, feeling every twitch, every response. Her skin was hot, flushed, her scent a mixture of sweat and arousal. The act—the sheer intimacy of it—sent a primal jolt through him. The submissive nature of it, the way she used them both for her pleasure, had his cock straining, harder than ever.

Rich, still buried between her thighs, sucked her clit into his mouth, flicking it with his tongue, and Ellie let out a strangled gasp, her knees trembling. "Oh, fuck—just like that," she moaned, her fingers tightening in his hair.

Her body was a masterpiece of sensation, her thighs quivering with each stroke of Rich's tongue, her stomach tightening with pleasure. Steve felt the way she clenched around nothing, the way her hips rocked back and forth, desperate for more.

Together, they worshipped her.

Rich moved lower, his tongue tracing along the entrance of her soaked pussy before plunging inside, drinking her in with greedy flicks. Steve, more confident now, spread her cheeks wider, delving deeper, his tongue moving in languid, teasing strokes.

Ellie's breathing grew heavier, her moans filling the room, harmonizing with the symphony of flesh on flesh. She rocked against them both, lost in the overwhelming pleasure of two men devoted to her body, each one desperate to push her over the edge.

Rich's fingers slid up her thighs, gripping them possessively, his tongue relentless. Steve's mouth worked with growing fervor, his lips pressing wet, open-mouthed kisses along the sensitive flesh, feeling her tremble beneath him.

Ellie's whole body burned. Every nerve was alive, pulsing, unraveling in pleasure.

Her orgasm hit hard. She threw her head back, her cry sharp and raw, her legs nearly buckling as waves of euphoria coursed through her. But they didn't stop. They didn't give her a second to recover.

Rich groaned against her, his hands gripping her hips tighter as he sucked her clit harder, as if chasing another orgasm before she could come down from the first. Steve, feeling her convulse above him, redoubled his efforts, his tongue working in urgent, hungry strokes.

"Oh—God, yes," Ellie sobbed, her nails digging into Rich's scalp as another climax crashed through her, stealing her breath, making her muscles go tight. Her entire body shuddered, her thighs clenching around Rich's face as she rode the pleasure out, her back arching.

Still, they didn't stop.

Steve, fully lost in the moment now, groaned into her, his own arousal unbearable. Rich was relentless, devouring her, his own cock dripping precum onto the floor, forgotten in his eagerness to make her come again.

Ellie's moans became incoherent, her words slurred with pleasure. Her body trembled violently as another climax tore through her, this one more intense than the last, leaving her gasping, wrecked, completely undone.

And then, finally, it was too much.

With a whimpering moan, she pulled away, her legs shaking as she stumbled back, collapsing onto the sofa, her body spent, glistening with sweat, her chest rising and falling in erratic breaths.

All eyes turned once more to Beth and Chloe, their bodies still writhing beneath the relentless thrusts of their lovers.

Ellie lay sprawled across the sofa, her body still tingling from the relentless pleasure she had just ridden out. Her skin glowed with a light sheen of sweat, her breath still uneven as she came down from the high. But she wasn't done enjoying herself—not yet.

With a slow, satisfied stretch, she sat up and patted the space on either side of her. "Come here," she murmured, her voice thick with lingering arousal.

Rich and Steve moved instantly, kneeling first, then settling onto the couch beside her. Their cocks stood hard and eager, flushed and glistening with precum, and Ellie wasted no time, curling her fingers around each of them, giving them a teasing, deliberate squeeze.

Rich exhaled a pleased sigh, sinking into the familiar comfort of her touch. He had been here before, he had been in this moment plenty of times, and he let himself relax into the pleasure of it, watching as Ellie's fingers slowly slid up and down his shaft, spreading the slickness of his arousal with each stroke.

Steve, however, was still reeling. Everything—the night, the situation, the surreal, all-consuming lust swirling inside him—felt like a fever dream. Ellie's hand around his cock was pure fire, her grip firm but unhurried, the slow drag of her palm along his length making his stomach clench with pleasure.

And then there was the view.

Across the room, Chloe was moaning, her body arching as George drove into her one last time, his thrusts erratic, desperate. Steve could see it all—the way her hands fisted in the sheets, the way her legs locked tight around him, pulling him deeper, urging him on.

Ellie's fingers squeezed around his shaft just as George let out a guttural groan, his entire body tensing as he buried himself inside Chloe and came. Steve could see the way George shuddered, the way Chloe gasped as she felt the heat of it flooding her, her body trembling in response.

A shiver ran through Steve, his cock twitching in Ellie's hand, but just as the pleasure coiled tight inside him, she slowed her strokes, pulling back just enough to keep him on the edge. He let out a shaky breath, his thighs clenching, desperate for more friction.

Ellie turned her head, watching him with a knowing smirk. "Not yet," she murmured, her thumb teasing over the sensitive head of his cock in the lightest, most infuriating way.

Steve groaned, his body tensed, but she was already shifting her attention back to the scene in front of them.

Chloe was panting, her body still trembling in George's arms, her legs loose and spent as he slowly withdrew. A slick mixture of cum and arousal glistened between her thighs, a lewd reminder of just how thoroughly she had been taken.

But the night wasn't over.

Beth was next.

Steve's breath hitched as he turned his attention to his wife, still pinned beneath Tommy, her face flushed, her lips parted in bliss.

Tommy was close, his body taut with restraint, his hips rolling in deep, slow thrusts, drawing out every last second before his release.

Ellie picked up her pace again, stroking Steve a little faster, a little firmer, her other hand moving just as skillfully over Rich.

Steve's head fell back against the couch, his jaw tightening as he fought against the growing tension in his core. His cock throbbed in her grasp, right on the edge of release.

And then he heard Beth's voice.

"Oh God, yes—"

She was close.

Steve forced his eyes open again, and the sight before him nearly broke him. Beth's body was writhing beneath Tommy, her fingers digging into his back, her legs trembling as he fucked her through the final stretch. She was lost in it, completely given over to the sensation, and Steve could do nothing but watch as Tommy groaned, burying himself deep one last time.

Ellie's grip tightened around Steve's cock at the exact moment Tommy let out a deep, guttural sound, his muscles locking as he came inside Beth. Steve saw it—the way his wife's body shuddered, the way her back arched, the soft, wrecked moan that spilled from her lips as she took every drop.

Steve's whole body tensed, the pleasure boiling over inside him, but just as he teetered on the edge, Ellie slowed her strokes again, squeezing the base of his cock, denying him the release that felt so unbearably close.

"Not yet," she whispered, her lips brushing against his ear.

Steve groaned in frustration, his entire body aching with the need to come, but Ellie just smirked, her fingers still moving in those slow, torturous strokes that kept him right at the precipice without ever letting him fall.

Then, across the room, Tommy finally pulled out of Beth.

There was a beat of silence.

And then Beth let out a massive, wet queef, the sound loud, raw, the first trickle of Tommy's cum oozing out of her swollen, well-used pussy.

Ellie chuckled, giving both men in her hands a teasing squeeze. "Well," she mused, her voice warm and amused. "That was something."

But she wasn't done with them yet.

Ellie stretched lazily, her body still buzzing with satisfaction as she surveyed the two men beside her, their cocks hard, desperate for release, still glistening from her touch. With a slow, knowing smirk, she sat up and patted their chests.

"Go lay on the bed," she commanded softly, her voice a mixture of sultry amusement and authority. "It's time for you to reclaim your wives."

Rich and Steve moved immediately, still caught in the thrall of her control, still burning from the pleasure she had denied them. They climbed onto the bed, lying side by side, their breaths uneven, their bodies tense with anticipation.

Ellie followed, settling between them, her presence electric.

Across the room, Chloe and Beth had finally caught their breath, their bodies still flushed, still trembling from their own ecstasy. Slowly, they began making their way toward the bed, their eyes heavy with arousal, their lips curled into satisfied, knowing smiles.

Rich's eyes locked on Chloe as she stepped closer, her movements slow and sensual, like she was savoring the moment.

But before Beth could reach Steve, Ellie moved.

With a wicked grin, she wrapped her fingers around Steve's cock, her grip tight, hot, relentless.

Steve gasped, his whole body jerking at the sudden contact.

She didn't ease him into it—she took control immediately, her hand working him in firm, fast strokes, her thumb sliding over the swollen head, smearing the precum that leaked freely.

Then she leaned in, her lips brushing against his ear, her breath hot as she whispered, her voice dripping with filth.

"Look at her, Steve," she murmured, her strokes quickening. "Look at your wife—walking toward you with another man's cum dripping out of her used little pussy."

Steve let out a strangled groan, his hips twitching involuntarily into Ellie's hand, his body betraying him completely.

"She's fucking full of it," Ellie purred, her tongue flicking over the shell of his ear. "So stretched out, so messy. Do you think she can even feel you after that?"

Steve's pulse roared in his ears. His cock throbbed furiously in Ellie's grasp, his stomach tightening, his balls drawing up, everything in him teetering on the very edge.

Beth climbed onto the bed, her bare skin glowing in the dim light, her legs still shaky.

And then—

Another queef.

Loud, shameless, lewd.

The sound filled the room, a perfect reminder of everything that had just been done to her body, of how thoroughly she had been taken, stretched, filled.

It was too much.

Ellie let out a husky, satisfied laugh, her hand moving in brutal, punishing strokes. "Fuck, there it is," she breathed. "Come for me, Steve. Come thinking about how wrecked your wife is."

Steve's entire body locked up, and with a hoarse, helpless cry, he came harder than he ever had in his life. His release exploded from him, thick, hot ropes spilling over his stomach, his chest, pulsing endlessly as his body convulsed beneath Ellie's unrelenting grip.

Beth gasped, her eyes widening at the sheer force of it, at how much he came, at how utterly ruined he looked in that moment.

And then, unexpectedly, she giggled.

It was small, breathy, surprised—but undeniably amused.

Ellie smirked, giving Steve's cock a final, teasing squeeze before letting go, watching him tremble in the aftermath of his climax.

She leaned back, stretching, completely satisfied with what she had done.

Rich exhaled a shaky breath, shaking his head with a smirk. "Damn."

Beth, still giggling softly, crawled closer, finally reaching for her husband, her fingers running over his heaving chest, her lips parting as she took in the absolute mess Ellie had made of him.

Steve's chest still heaved from the force of his orgasm, his skin damp with sweat, his stomach a mess of his own release. He barely had time to recover before Beth crawled over him, her body still warm and flushed from the night's endless pleasure.

He could see the way her thighs trembled, the way her breath hitched, the way her eyes gleamed with something new—something powerful.

She knew what she wanted now.

She straddled his chest, her hands on his shoulders, and Steve could see it—see the mess between her legs, the slick, swollen folds still leaking with Tommy's thick load.

And she wanted him to clean her.

His stomach lurched at the thought.

No.

Not this.

He shook his head, hands instinctively coming up to push at her hips, his heart pounding. "Beth, I—"

She didn't move.

Her thighs caged him in, and though she wasn't forcing herself down on him yet, she simply waited.

"You've watched me take another man's cum," she murmured, her voice strangely soft, almost teasing. "You've watched me be stretched, filled, used. You know what's dripping out of me, don't you, Steve?"

His throat tightened.

She wasn't making him—she was letting him make the decision himself.

But the longer he hesitated, the longer he fought it, the more humiliating it became.

His cock, despite being drained, twitched at the power she suddenly had over him.

A shift in dynamic.

A reversal.

Beth had already submitted tonight. She had swallowed another man's cum, even though it disgusted her. She had taken pleasure in it, in the powerlessness, in the way it made her feel owned.

Now, it was his turn.

She lowered herself.

Steve groaned, turning his head to the side, his hands still weakly pressing at her thighs, a last attempt to delay the inevitable.

She leaned down, her lips brushing his ear.

"Lick it up."

Then she sat down on his face.

The heat, the scent, the taste—it was overwhelming. Wrong.

Steve tried to fight it, but she rolled her hips, pressing herself against his lips, smearing Tommy's cum against his mouth, making sure he felt how much was still inside her.

His mind screamed at him to resist.

But Beth had found herself tonight.

She had discovered the power in surrender, in giving herself over to something that both disgusted and excited her.

Now, she wanted Steve to understand it, too.

She ground down on him, her hands threading through his hair, holding him in place.

"Do it," she whispered. "Lick me clean."

His tongue trembled as it finally flicked against her, hesitant, weak. The first taste of her, of them, sent a violent shudder through his body. It wasn't just Beth—it was Tommy. The thickness of it. The sheer amount of it.

It was too much.

He could feel it dripping onto his tongue.

Then he heard Chloe moan.

His eyes darted to the side, barely able to focus, but the sight made his stomach twist with jealousy.

Chloe was riding Rich, her body moving in slow, sensual rolls, her head thrown back, lost in her own pleasure.

And Rich—Rich was still hard.

Steve clenched his fists.

Rich hadn't embarrassed himself. He hadn't lost control. He was still strong, still fucking, still commanding his wife's pleasure while Steve was here, trapped beneath Beth, licking up another man's cum.

Beth felt the shift in him—the moment of resentment—and it excited her.

"You don't like that, do you?" she whispered, grinding harder, forcing more of it out. "You hate that he's still fucking while you're—"

She squeezed her pussy around his tongue.

A loud, wet queef.

And with it—a fresh load of cum dribbled into his mouth.

Steve whimpered.

His hips twitched, the last shreds of his resistance breaking.

Beth moaned, feeling his surrender, feeling his tongue finally move with purpose.

He wasn't just tolerating it now.

He was licking.

Tasting.

Submitting.

She rolled off him, onto her back, spreading her legs wide, her hands gripping her own thighs as she gave herself to him completely.

"Keep going."

This was different now.

He wasn't trapped beneath her.

He could stop at any time.

But he didn't.

He dove back in, his tongue flicking over her swollen clit, his mouth sealing around her, taking her in willingly now.

His face was soaked, his lips sticky, his own body shuddering at the sheer depravity of what he was doing.

And Beth loved it.

She tugged his hair roughly, yanking him in harder, her thighs trembling as pleasure built.

Then she heard it.

Another moan.

Chloe again—but this time, she wasn't on Rich's cock.

Steve's eyes flickered to the side just in time to see Chloe straddling Rich's face.

Her head was tilted back, her hands gripping the headboard, riding his mouth, her thighs clenched tight around his head.

Steve's cock, somehow, unbelievably, twitched back to life.

Beth saw it.

She felt it.

She yanked his hair hard, pulling him right into her at the exact moment her orgasm ripped through her.

She screamed, her whole body shaking, her thighs pressing against Steve's head as she rode his tongue through the most intense climax of her life.

Steve groaned against her, tasting everything, feeling everything, his world reduced to nothing but Beth's pleasure, her taste, her scent, the way her body claimed him.

Then—finally—she collapsed back against the bed, breathless, sated.

The room was silent except for heavy breathing, the lingering pulse of bodies still coming down.

Then, from the other side of the bed, Chloe let out a breathy, satisfied laugh.

"Fuck," she murmured, stretching. "We really are some slutty bitches."

Beth giggled breathlessly, shaking her head. "No kidding."

Ellie, lounging on the edge of the bed, smirked. "I was gonna say something, but I figured you all already knew."

Laughter rippled through the group, the air shifting, the intensity melting into something warm, teasing, familiar.

Then, one by one, they started gathering their things, pulling on crumpled clothing, adjusting hair, catching each other's eyes in the soft glow of the bedside lamp.

Ellie and George remained as the others filtered out.

The taxi ride back to Chloe and Rich's was surreal.

No one spoke about what had just happened.

There was no awkwardness, no shame—just normal conversation.

A joke about the driver's terrible music choice.

A casual comment about how late it was.

It was like any other night out with friends.

Except Steve could still taste Beth on his tongue.

And they all knew.

This wasn't the last time.

Not even close.

When they finally arrived back at Chloe and Rich's place, there were no lingering glances, no unspoken words—just the heavy weight of exhaustion settling over them like a thick blanket. Clothes were peeled off in silence, bodies moving on autopilot as they climbed into bed, the warmth of familiar sheets wrapping around them. There was no energy left for anything more, no whispered confessions or playful touches. Just deep, satisfied exhaustion. Within moments, they were asleep, tangled in the remnants of the night, their bodies still humming with everything they had done—but their minds finally at rest.

THE FINAL MOMENT

The next morning, the four of them woke late, stretching off the lingering aches of the night before. It was far too late for breakfast, so they settled for a long, lazy brunch instead. Their night out had lasted until nearly three in the morning, and by the time they'd stumbled into bed, sleep had claimed them instantly, exhaustion overtaking even the last flickers of arousal.

As Steve poured coffee, he handed the pot to Rich, who barely mustered the strength to take it.

"How's your head?" Steve asked, smirking at the rough shape his friend was in.

"Not too good right now," Rich admitted with a groan. "I'm just glad you were still okay to drive us home. I don't think I would've made it."

"We all kind of overdid it, huh?" Chloe chuckled, stretching her arms over her head before wincing slightly. "I'm a bit sore and definitely hungover, but I'll be fine in a few hours."

Beth nodded, staring into her coffee cup as if it might hold some answers. "That was… definitely more than I planned on," she admitted. "I still can't believe I managed to take on three men in such a short time. I don't even know what came over me."

Steve slid his arm around his wife's waist, pulling her close as he kissed the top of her head. "You were incredible, Beth. I don't think I've ever been so turned on in my life, watching you let go like that, taking so much pleasure."

Beth hesitated, biting her lip. "You don't think I'm... a wanton slut now, do you? I mean, the last few days were so out of character for me."

Steve squeezed her tighter. "Hell no! This trip took both of us into uncharted territory, sure. But I wouldn't change a thing. If anything, I think we should be thanking Chloe and Rich. They helped us open up, not just to others, but to ourselves. This wasn't just a fantasy anymore. We actually lived it. And I just hope you feel the same way I do."

Beth lifted her gaze to his, her eyes misty. Then she turned to Chloe, a slow, warm smile spreading across her face. "Oh, honey, I do. I don't think I've ever felt so alive as I did last night. Even though I was hesitant at first, once I let go... it was amazing. If we never do anything like this again, I'll still always remember those feelings." She chuckled, shaking her head. "I really did let it all hang out—literally."

Chloe beamed. "We're just happy you both had such a great time," she said. "And I hope this isn't the last time we all get together for a little fun."

Beth raised a brow. "Oh, it won't be. But next time, it's your turn to visit us. I don't know if we can match the kind of club scene you introduced us to, but I have a feeling we'll find plenty of ways to keep things exciting." She shot Steve a knowing look. "And I'm pretty sure Steve is looking forward to spending more time with you, Chloe."

As they finished their coffee, Rich got up and stretched. "Well, if we're nursing hangovers, I say we do it properly. Bloody Marys and a soak in the hot tub?"

"Now that's an idea I can get behind," Beth agreed, already feeling the tension in her muscles.

A half-hour later, the four of them were once again nude, steam rising around them as they lounged in and around the hot tub. The water soothed their sore bodies, but it wasn't long before hands started wandering.

Steve had Beth bent over the edge, his slow, deliberate thrusts drawing soft moans from her lips as the warm water lapped at their skin. Nearby, Rich sat on a stool, watching as Chloe, with a wicked smile, eased herself down onto his cock, working him into her tight heat inch by inch. The erotic scene unfolded around them, a final indulgence before the inevitable goodbye.

Later, as Beth stepped out of the tub and wrapped a thick towel around herself, Chloe approached her. Without hesitation, she pulled Beth into her arms, their lips meeting in a slow, lingering kiss. Their bodies pressed together, nipples brushing as they melted into the moment, sharing one last taste of the night before.

By the afternoon, Steve and Beth were packed, their bags loaded into the car.

They lingered in the driveway, reluctant to say goodbye.

"Call me next week," Chloe said, hugging Beth one last time. "We need to start planning the next time we can do this."

Beth smiled, her fingers lightly tracing Chloe's arm. "That's a deal. And maybe next time, I'll have built up the courage to return a few of the favors you gave me."

Chloe grinned. "I'll hold you to that."

As Steve and Beth pulled away, watching Rich and Chloe wave

from the driveway, the entire weekend felt like a surreal, intoxicating dream.

The ride home was quiet.

No one mentioned what had happened, though the memories lingered between them like a silent electric current. Instead, they talked about normal things—plans for the week, mundane details of life—just like old friends after a wild night out.

But deep down, they both knew.

This wasn't the last time.

Not even close.

The End

BOOKS BY THIS AUTHOR

Shared In Sin City: A Couple's Journey

As Lucy looked out of the rented Mustang's windows, she saw that famous sign: Welcome to Las Vegas. She knew the weekend was going to be fun—who has a dull time in Vegas, right?

In fact, she'd been planning to make this trip a little wilder than usual for her and Chris. But as she glanced at her husband in the driver's seat, she could never have known how the weekend—and their lives—would end up taking such a dramatic turn.

She had no idea they were about to meet James and Emily, and that a chance encounter was all it would take to change everything.

Chris never would have imagined he'd find himself sitting there, watching his wife on her knees, pleasuring another man—his mind screaming stop, but his body begging don't you dare stop.

Of course, that might have had something to do with Emily's head bobbing up and down in his lap.

A couple of wives sharing drinks in Vegas and giving each other's husbands a quick blowjob? That's one thing. But watching your wife naked, surrounded by strangers, stretched out by a random guy's massive cock? That's a completely different ball game. And for whatever reason, James seems perfectly happy to watch Emily in that position.

But not Lucy. She wouldn't go that far. Would she?

The sign might say Welcome to Las Vegas, but it really should say Welcome to Sin City.

Shared For The First Time: A Couple's Introduction To A New World

When Gemma booked this vacation, everything seemed so normal—just the two of us, my best friend Steve, and his wife, Charlotte. We all got along great, so what could possibly go wrong?

But nothing could have prepared me for the moment I looked over and saw my best friend's face buried between my wife's legs. I know what you're thinking—I should have been angry. I should have stopped them.

And I probably would have... if I hadn't just cum in Charlotte's mouth.

But I know what you're thinking. This was all planned, some elaborate scheme one of us had set up. The truth, though, is much simpler—a little too much to drink, a little too much sun, and a handjob.

This is how we shared for the first time.

Swap: A Ski Trip With A Difference

Even a week ago, I never would have imagined this could have happened. Looking up and watching my wife's head bobbing up and down in my friend's lap. Well, actually that part I could imagine, we've played a little bit before.

But what I couldn't have imagined was Emma, on her knees in front of me, doing the same. Shy, innocent Emma. I never had the slightest idea she had it in her!

Although it's fair to say she definitely has it in her now!

But there's a final step or two, and I don't just want to enjoy Emma, I want to watch my wife enjoy her too. There's only one question left to answer. Was it really fear in her eyes the moment Lucy's mouth moved in to kiss her?

Okay, it was definitely fear, I won't lie. She was terrified, shaking, breathing fast, almost in shock. But the rock hard nipples were another part of the same story. The fear might have been fear she was about to enjoy it!

Nothing could have prepared either of them for this, but then again, what can ever prepare a married couple for their introduction into the world of swinging?

Printed in Dunstable, United Kingdom